W9-AHG-891

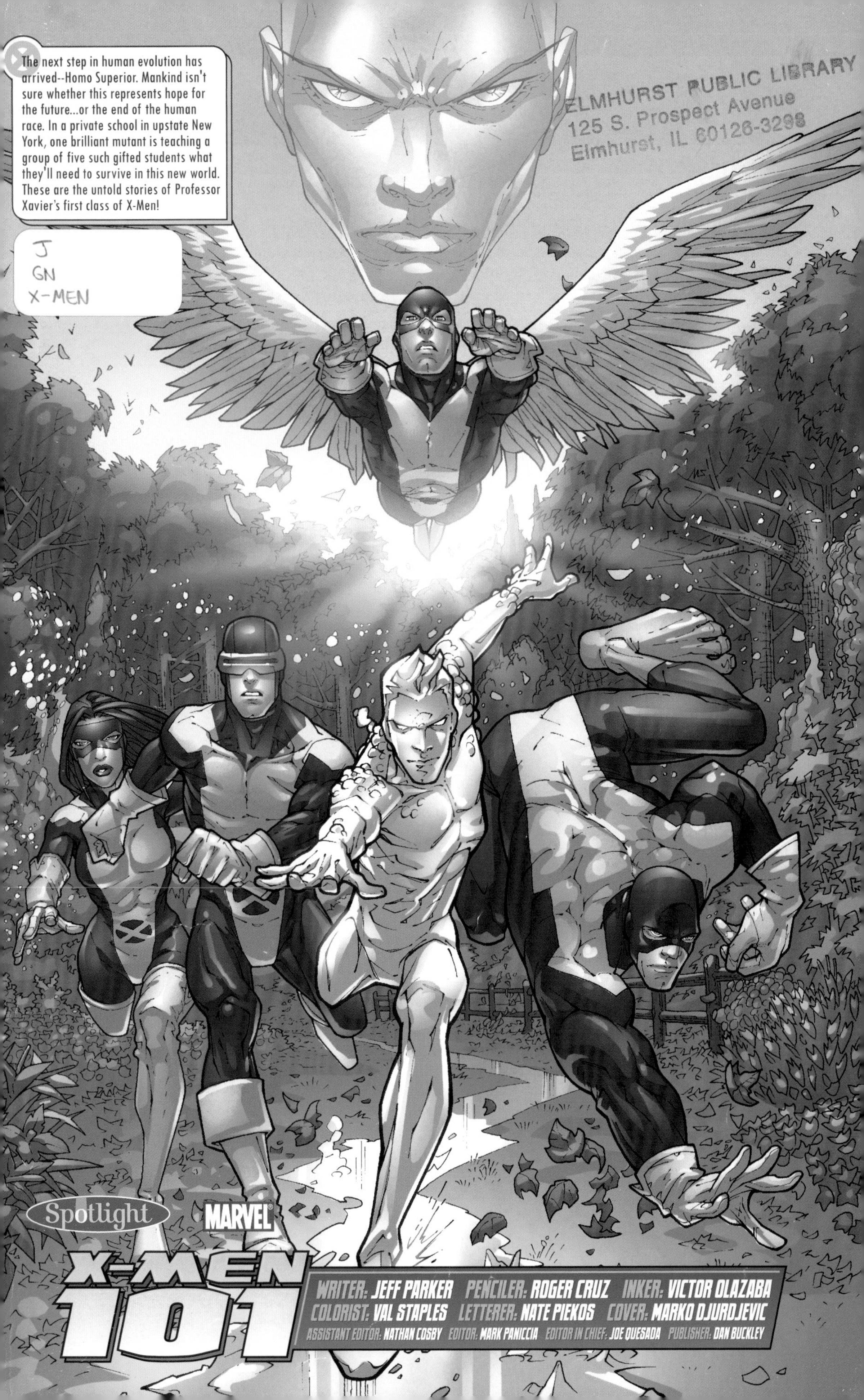
The next step in human evolution has arrived--Homo Superior. Mankind isn't sure whether this represents hope for the future...or the end of the human race. In a private school in upstate New York, one brilliant mutant is teaching a group of five such gifted students what they'll need to survive in this new world. These are the untold stories of Professor Xavier's first class of X-Men!
Spotlight
MARVEL
X-MEN 101
WRITER: JEFF PARKER PENCILER: ROGER CRUZ INKER: VICTOR OLAZABA
COLORIST: VAL STAPLES LETTERER: NATE PIEKOS COVER: MARKO DJURDJEVIC
ASSISTANT EDITOR: NATHAN COSBY EDITOR: MARK PANICCIA EDITOR IN CHIEF: JOE QUESADA PUBLISHER: DAN BUCKLEY

VISIT US AT
www.abdopublishing.com

Reinforced library bound edition published in 2008 by Spotlight, a division of the ABDO Publishing Group, 8000 West 78th Street, Edina, Minnesota 55439. Spotlight produces high-quality reinforced library bound editions for schools and libraries. Published by agreement with Marvel Characters, Inc.

Library of Congress Cataloging-in-Publication Data

Parker, Jeff, 1966-
  X-Men 101 / writer, Jeff Parker ; penciler, Roger Cruz ; inker, Victor Olazaba ; colorist, Val Staples ; letterer, Nate Piekos ; cover, Marko Djurdjevic. -- Reinforced library bound ed.
      p. cm. -- (X-Men)
  "Marvel age"--Cover.
  Revision of issue 1 of X-Men.
  ISBN 978-1-59961-401-4
  1. Graphic novels. I. Cruz, Roger. II. X-Men (New York, N.Y. : 2004). 1. III. Title. IV. Title: X-Men one hundred one. V. Title: X-Men one-oh-one. VI. Title: X-Men one-o-one.

PN6728.X2P39 2008
741.5'973--dc22

                                                              2007020250

All Spotlight books have reinforced library bindings and
are manufactured in the United States of America.

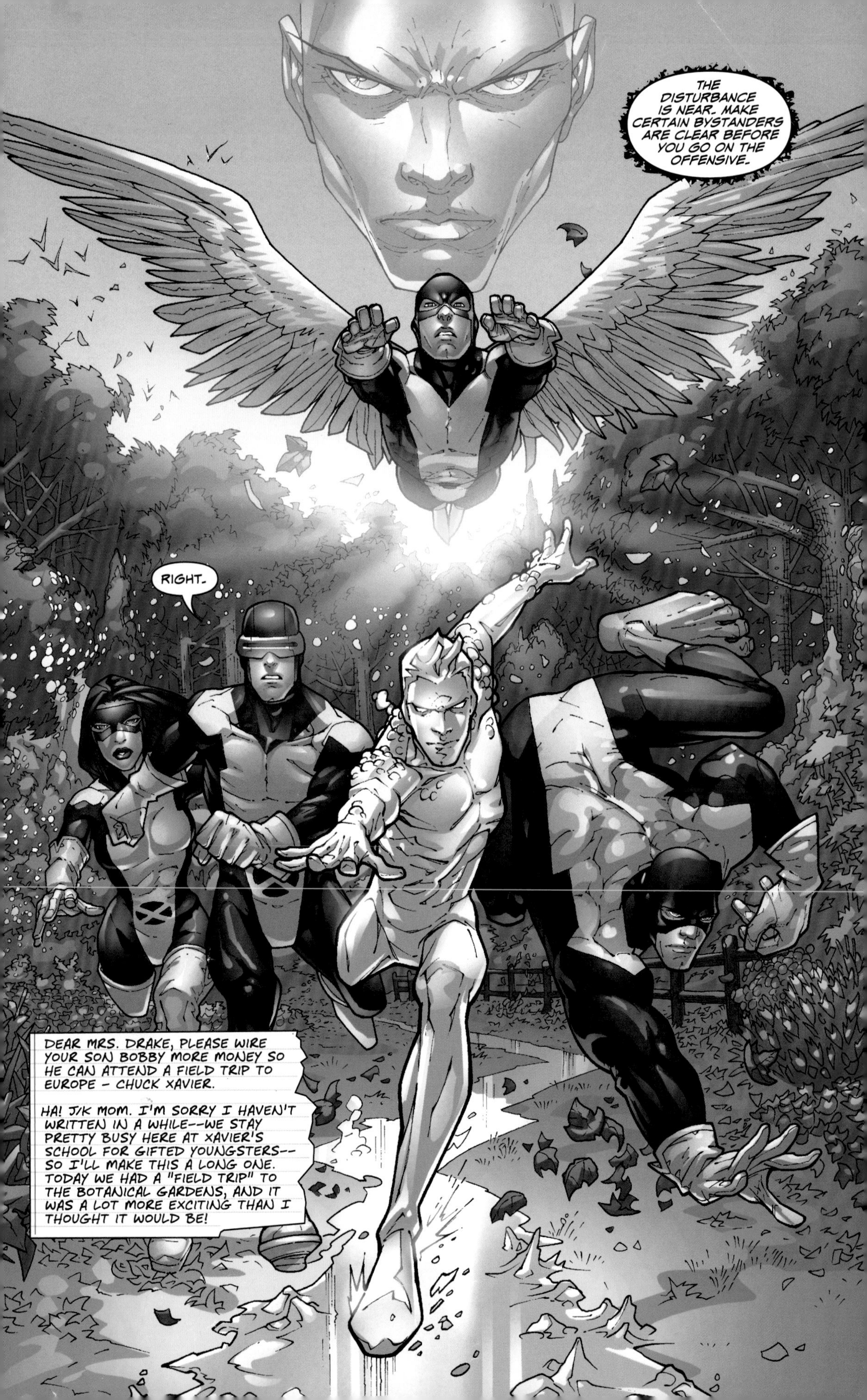
THE DISTURBANCE IS NEAR. MAKE CERTAIN BYSTANDERS ARE CLEAR BEFORE YOU GO ON THE OFFENSIVE.
RIGHT.
DEAR MRS. DRAKE, PLEASE WIRE YOUR SON BOBBY MORE MONEY SO HE CAN ATTEND A FIELD TRIP TO EUROPE - CHUCK XAVIER.
HA! J/K MOM. I'M SORRY I HAVEN'T WRITTEN IN A WHILE--WE STAY PRETTY BUSY HERE AT XAVIER'S SCHOOL FOR GIFTED YOUNGSTERS--SO I'LL MAKE THIS A LONG ONE. TODAY WE HAD A "FIELD TRIP" TO THE BOTANICAL GARDENS, AND IT WAS A LOT MORE EXCITING THAN I THOUGHT IT WOULD BE!

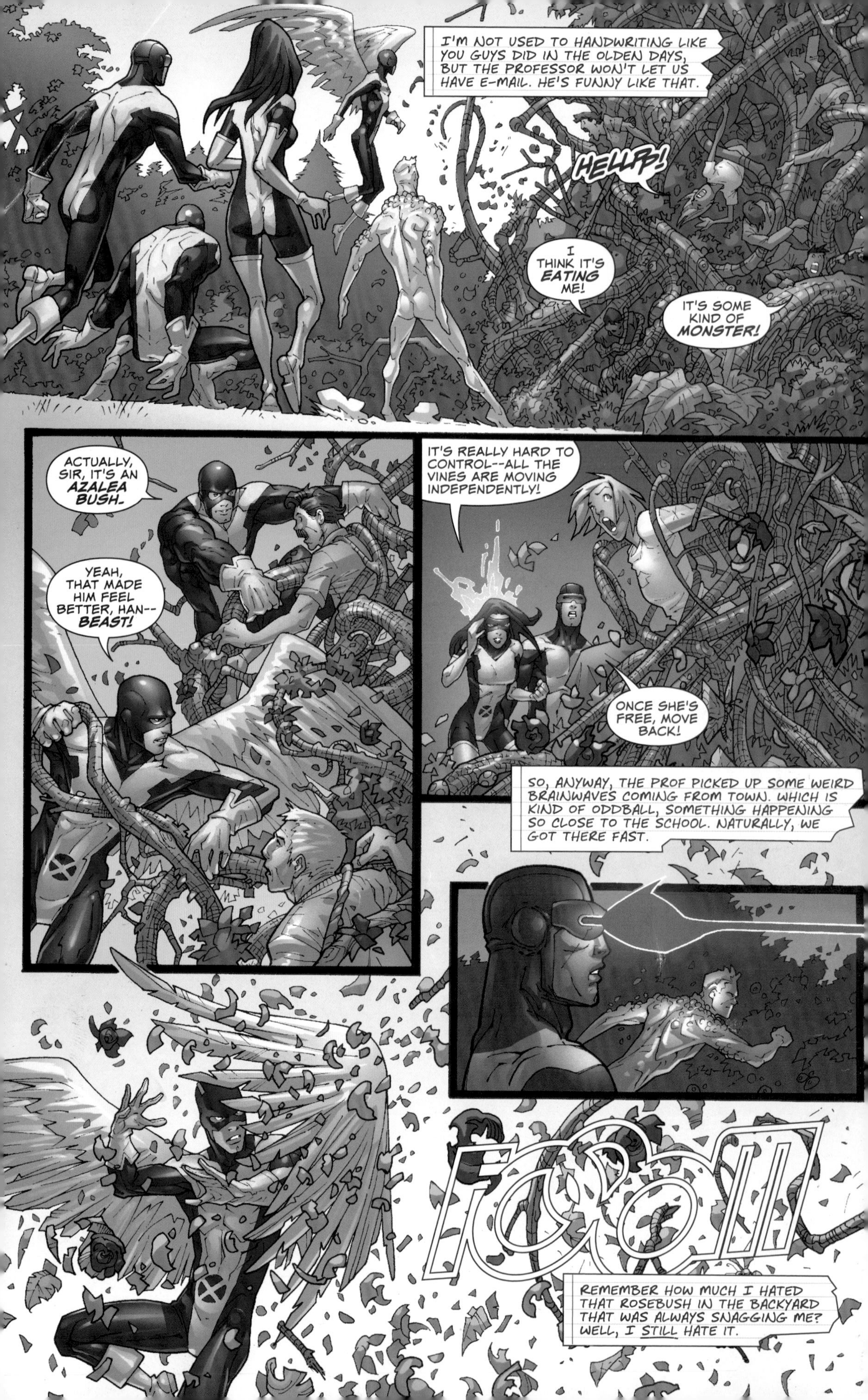
I'M NOT USED TO HANDWRITING LIKE YOU GUYS DID IN THE OLDEN DAYS, BUT THE PROFESSOR WON'T LET US HAVE E-MAIL. HE'S FUNNY LIKE THAT.
HELLLP!
I THINK IT'S EATING ME!
IT'S SOME KIND OF MONSTER!
ACTUALLY, SIR, IT'S AN AZALEA BUSH.
YEAH, THAT MADE HIM FEEL BETTER, HAN--BEAST!
IT'S REALLY HARD TO CONTROL--ALL THE VINES ARE MOVING INDEPENDENTLY!
ONCE SHE'S FREE, MOVE BACK!
SO, ANYWAY, THE PROF PICKED UP SOME WEIRD BRAINWAVES COMING FROM TOWN. WHICH IS KIND OF ODDBALL, SOMETHING HAPPENING SO CLOSE TO THE SCHOOL. NATURALLY, WE GOT THERE FAST.
FOOM
REMEMBER HOW MUCH I HATED THAT ROSEBUSH IN THE BACKYARD THAT WAS ALWAYS SNAGGING ME? WELL, I STILL HATE IT.

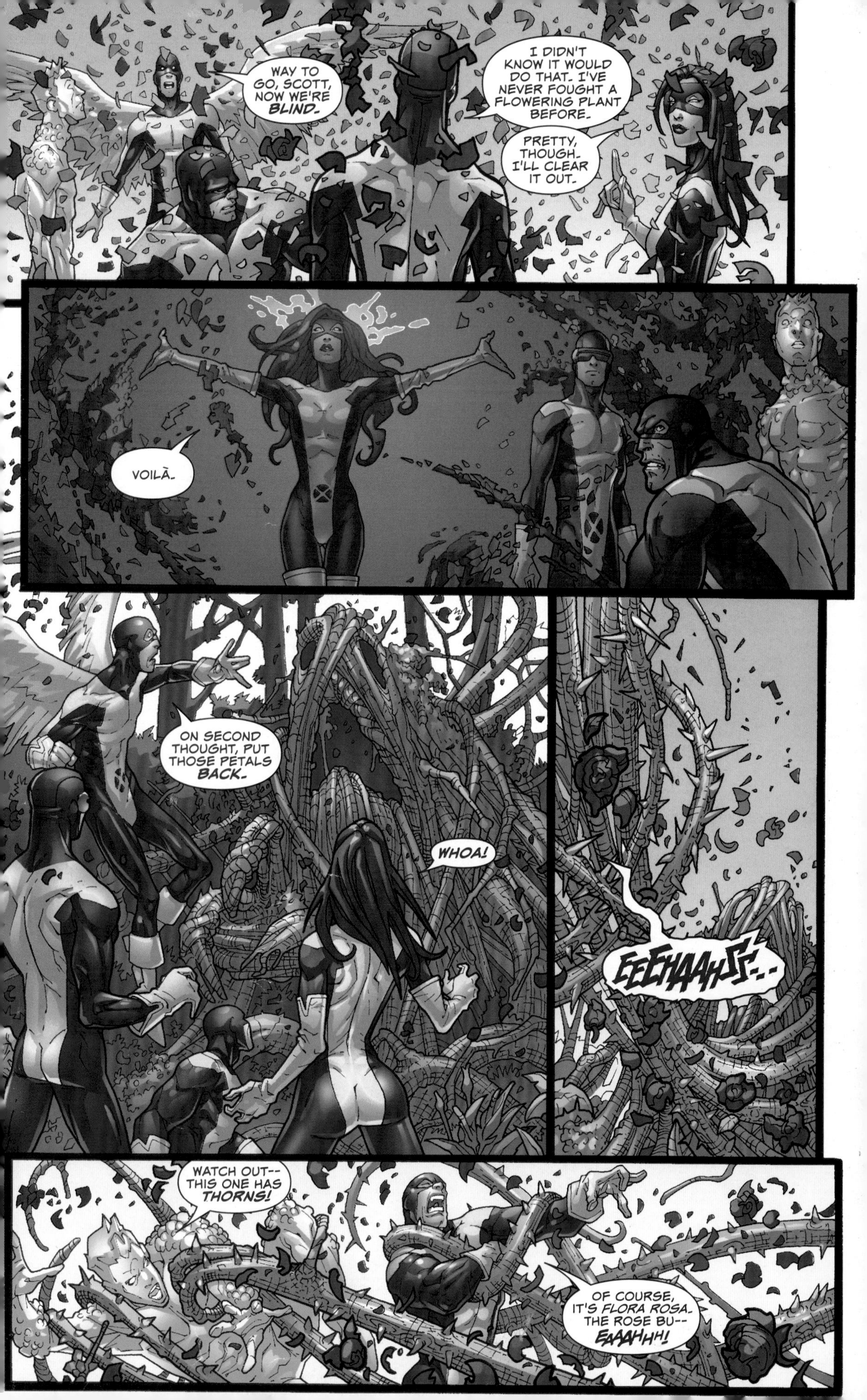

WAY TO GO, SCOTT, NOW WE'RE BLIND.
I DIDN'T KNOW IT WOULD DO THAT. I'VE NEVER FOUGHT A FLOWERING PLANT BEFORE.
PRETTY, THOUGH. I'LL CLEAR IT OUT.
VOILÀ.
ON SECOND THOUGHT, PUT THOSE PETALS BACK.
WHOA!
EEEHAAAHSSS...
WATCH OUT-- THIS ONE HAS THORNS!
OF COURSE, IT'S FLORA ROSA. THE ROSE BU-- EAAAHHH!

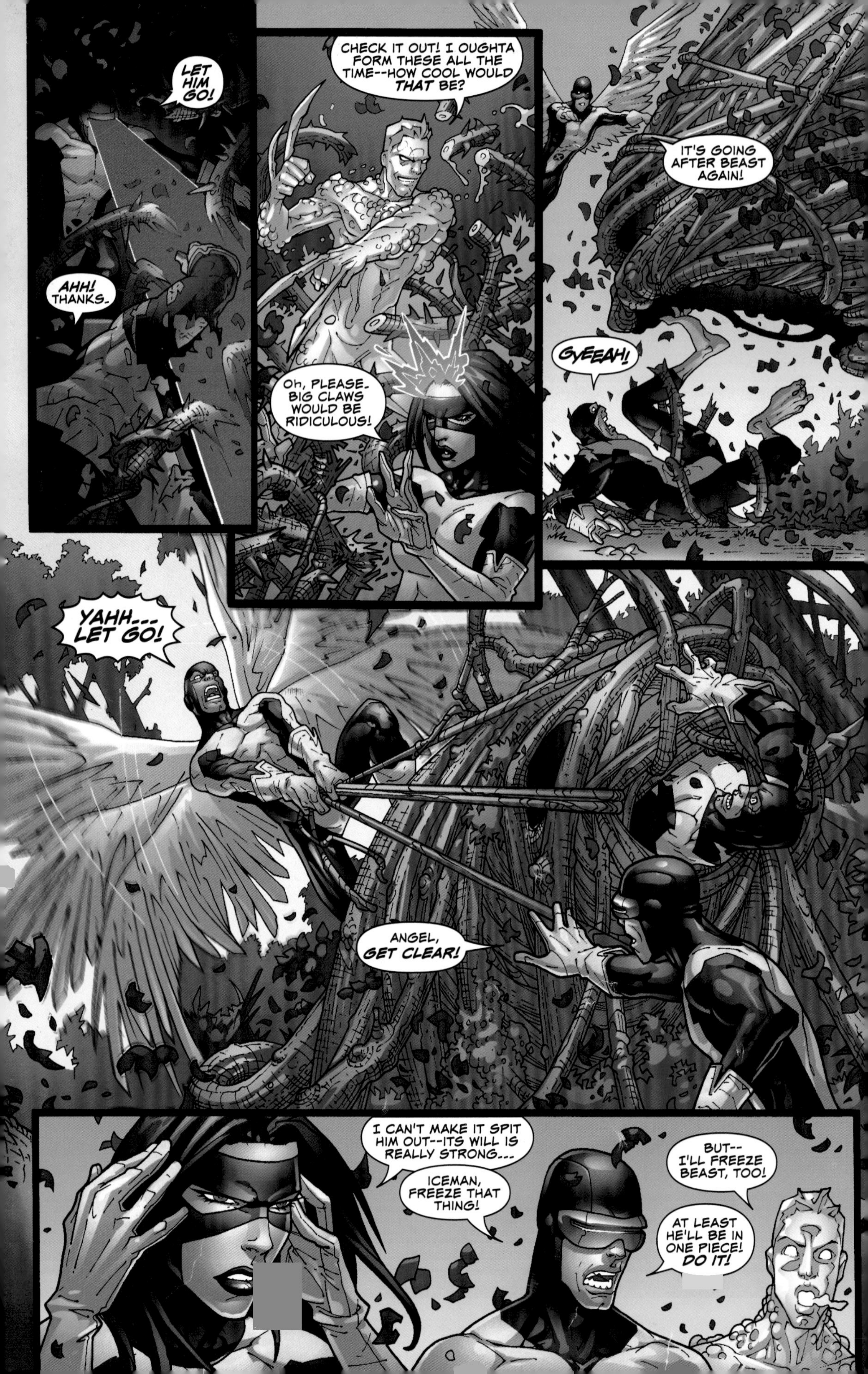
LET HIM GO!
AHH! THANKS.
CHECK IT OUT! I OUGHTA FORM THESE ALL THE TIME--HOW COOL WOULD THAT BE?
Oh, PLEASE. BIG CLAWS WOULD BE RIDICULOUS!
IT'S GOING AFTER BEAST AGAIN!
GYEEAH!
YAHH... LET GO!
ANGEL, GET CLEAR!
I CAN'T MAKE IT SPIT HIM OUT--ITS WILL IS REALLY STRONG...
ICEMAN, FREEZE THAT THING!
BUT-- I'LL FREEZE BEAST, TOO!
AT LEAST HE'LL BE IN ONE PIECE! DO IT!

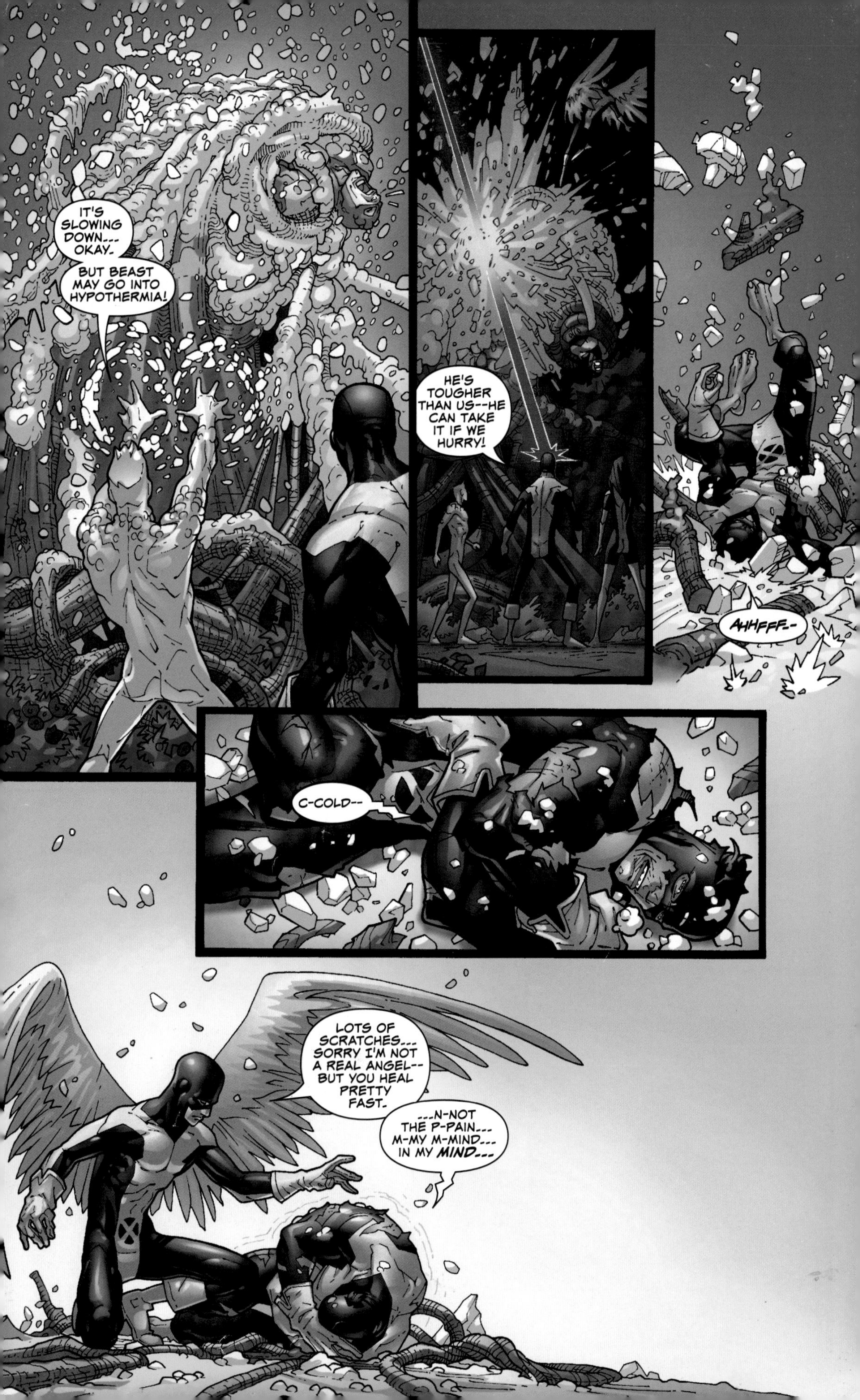
IT'S SLOWING DOWN... OKAY.
BUT BEAST MAY GO INTO HYPOTHERMIA!
HE'S TOUGHER THAN US--HE CAN TAKE IT IF WE HURRY!
AHHFFF.-
C-COLD--
LOTS OF SCRATCHES... SORRY I'M NOT A REAL ANGEL--BUT YOU HEAL PRETTY FAST.
...N-NOT THE P-PAIN... M-MY M-MIND... IN MY MIND...

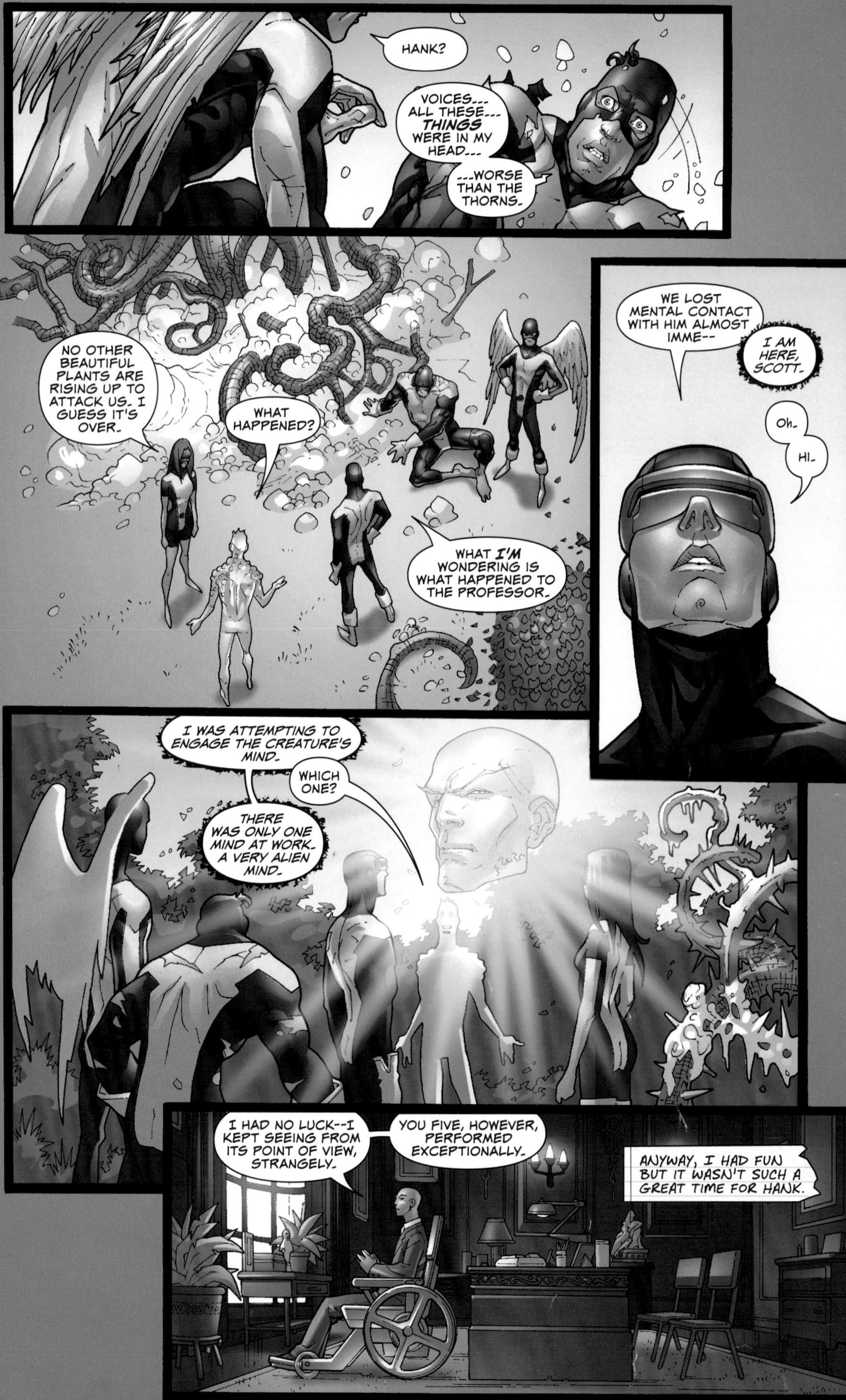
HANK?
VOICES... ALL THESE... THINGS WERE IN MY HEAD...
...WORSE THAN THE THORNS.
NO OTHER BEAUTIFUL PLANTS ARE RISING UP TO ATTACK US. I GUESS IT'S OVER.
WHAT HAPPENED?
WHAT I'M WONDERING IS WHAT HAPPENED TO THE PROFESSOR.
WE LOST MENTAL CONTACT WITH HIM ALMOST IMME--
I AM HERE, SCOTT.
Oh.
HI.
I WAS ATTEMPTING TO ENGAGE THE CREATURE'S MIND.
WHICH ONE?
THERE WAS ONLY ONE MIND AT WORK. A VERY ALIEN MIND.
I HAD NO LUCK--I KEPT SEEING FROM ITS POINT OF VIEW, STRANGELY.
YOU FIVE, HOWEVER, PERFORMED EXCEPTIONALLY.
ANYWAY, I HAD FUN BUT IT WASN'T SUCH A GREAT TIME FOR HANK.

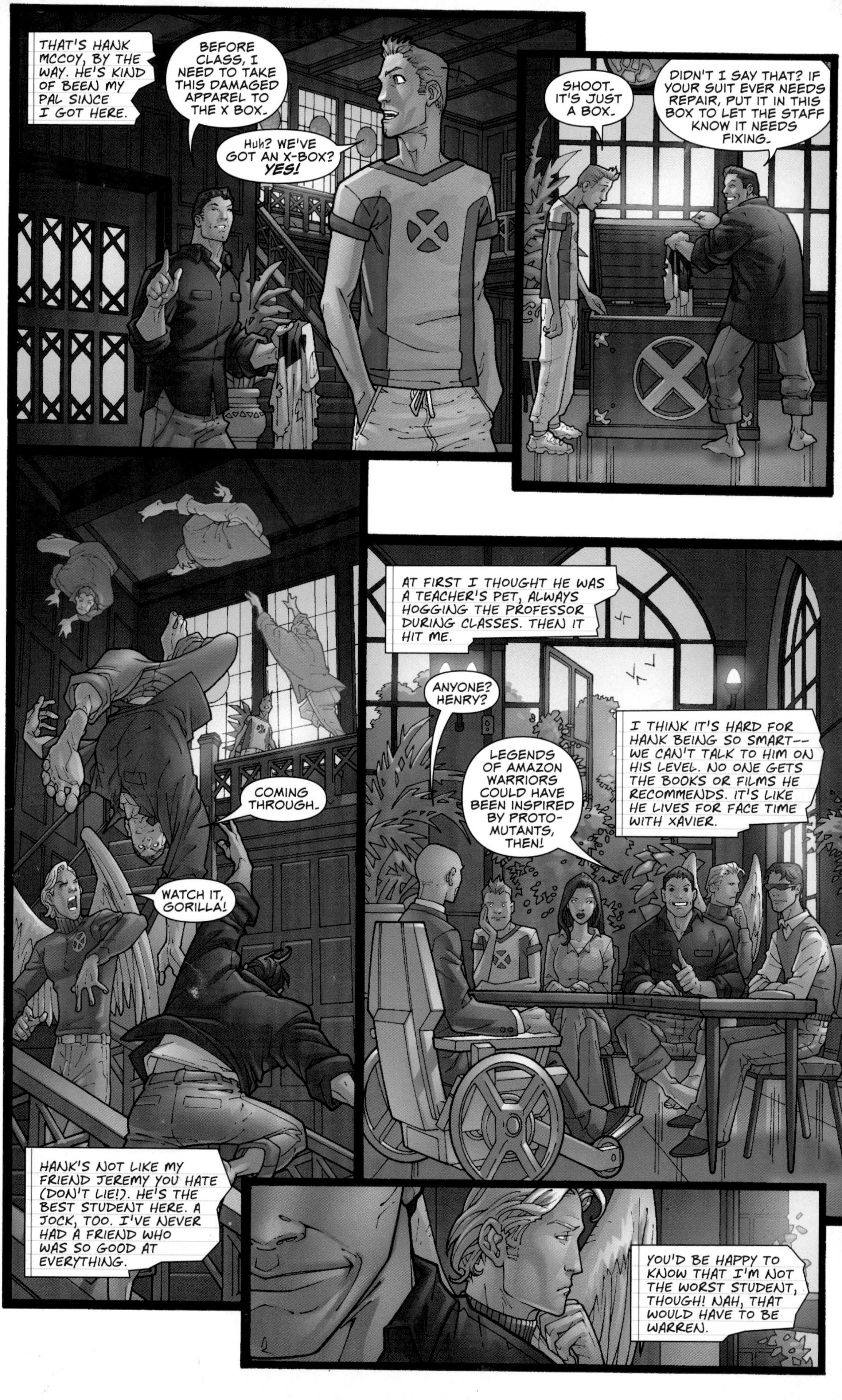

THAT'S HANK McCOY, BY THE WAY. HE'S KIND OF BEEN MY PAL SINCE I GOT HERE.
BEFORE CLASS, I NEED TO TAKE THIS DAMAGED APPAREL TO THE X BOX.
Huh? WE'VE GOT AN X-BOX? YES!
SHOOT. IT'S JUST A BOX.
DIDN'T I SAY THAT? IF YOUR SUIT EVER NEEDS REPAIR, PUT IT IN THIS BOX TO LET THE STAFF KNOW IT NEEDS FIXING.
COMING THROUGH.
WATCH IT, GORILLA!
HANK'S NOT LIKE MY FRIEND JEREMY YOU HATE (DON'T LIE!). HE'S THE BEST STUDENT HERE. A JOCK, TOO. I'VE NEVER HAD A FRIEND WHO WAS SO GOOD AT EVERYTHING.
AT FIRST I THOUGHT HE WAS A TEACHER'S PET, ALWAYS HOGGING THE PROFESSOR DURING CLASSES. THEN IT HIT ME.
ANYONE? HENRY?
LEGENDS OF AMAZON WARRIORS COULD HAVE BEEN INSPIRED BY PROTO-MUTANTS, THEN!
I THINK IT'S HARD FOR HANK BEING SO SMART-- WE CAN'T TALK TO HIM ON HIS LEVEL. NO ONE GETS THE BOOKS OR FILMS HE RECOMMENDS. IT'S LIKE HE LIVES FOR FACE TIME WITH XAVIER.
YOU'D BE HAPPY TO KNOW THAT I'M NOT THE WORST STUDENT, THOUGH! NAH, THAT WOULD HAVE TO BE WARREN.

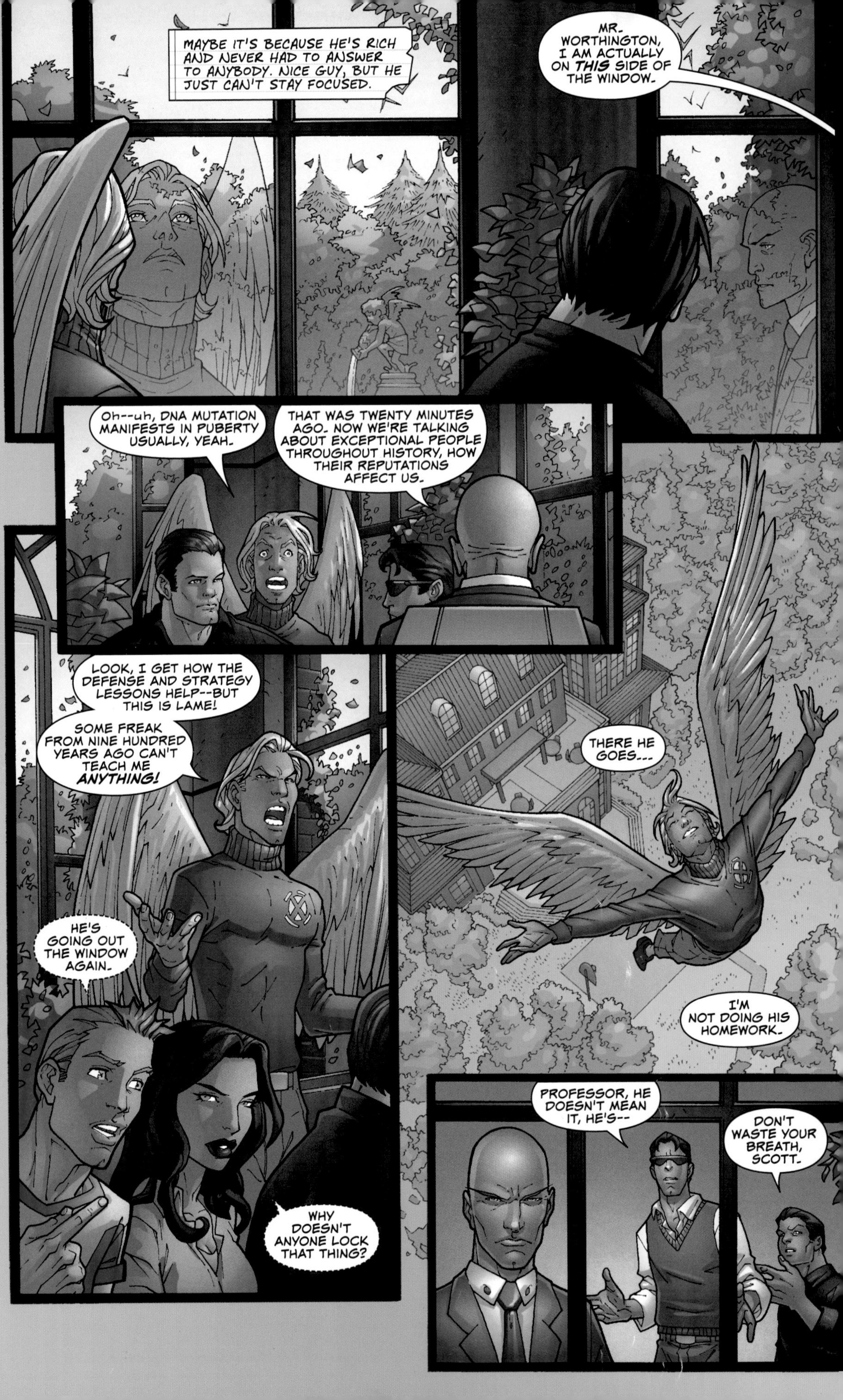
MAYBE IT'S BECAUSE HE'S RICH AND NEVER HAD TO ANSWER TO ANYBODY. NICE GUY, BUT HE JUST CAN'T STAY FOCUSED.
MR. WORTHINGTON, I AM ACTUALLY ON *THIS* SIDE OF THE WINDOW.
Oh--uh, DNA MUTATION MANIFESTS IN PUBERTY USUALLY, YEAH.
THAT WAS TWENTY MINUTES AGO. NOW WE'RE TALKING ABOUT EXCEPTIONAL PEOPLE THROUGHOUT HISTORY, HOW THEIR REPUTATIONS AFFECT US.
LOOK, I GET HOW THE DEFENSE AND STRATEGY LESSONS HELP--BUT THIS IS LAME!
SOME FREAK FROM NINE HUNDRED YEARS AGO CAN'T TEACH ME ***ANYTHING!***
HE'S GOING OUT THE WINDOW AGAIN.
WHY DOESN'T ANYONE LOCK THAT THING?
THERE HE GOES...
I'M NOT DOING HIS HOMEWORK.
PROFESSOR, HE DOESN'T MEAN IT, HE'S--
DON'T WASTE YOUR BREATH, SCOTT.

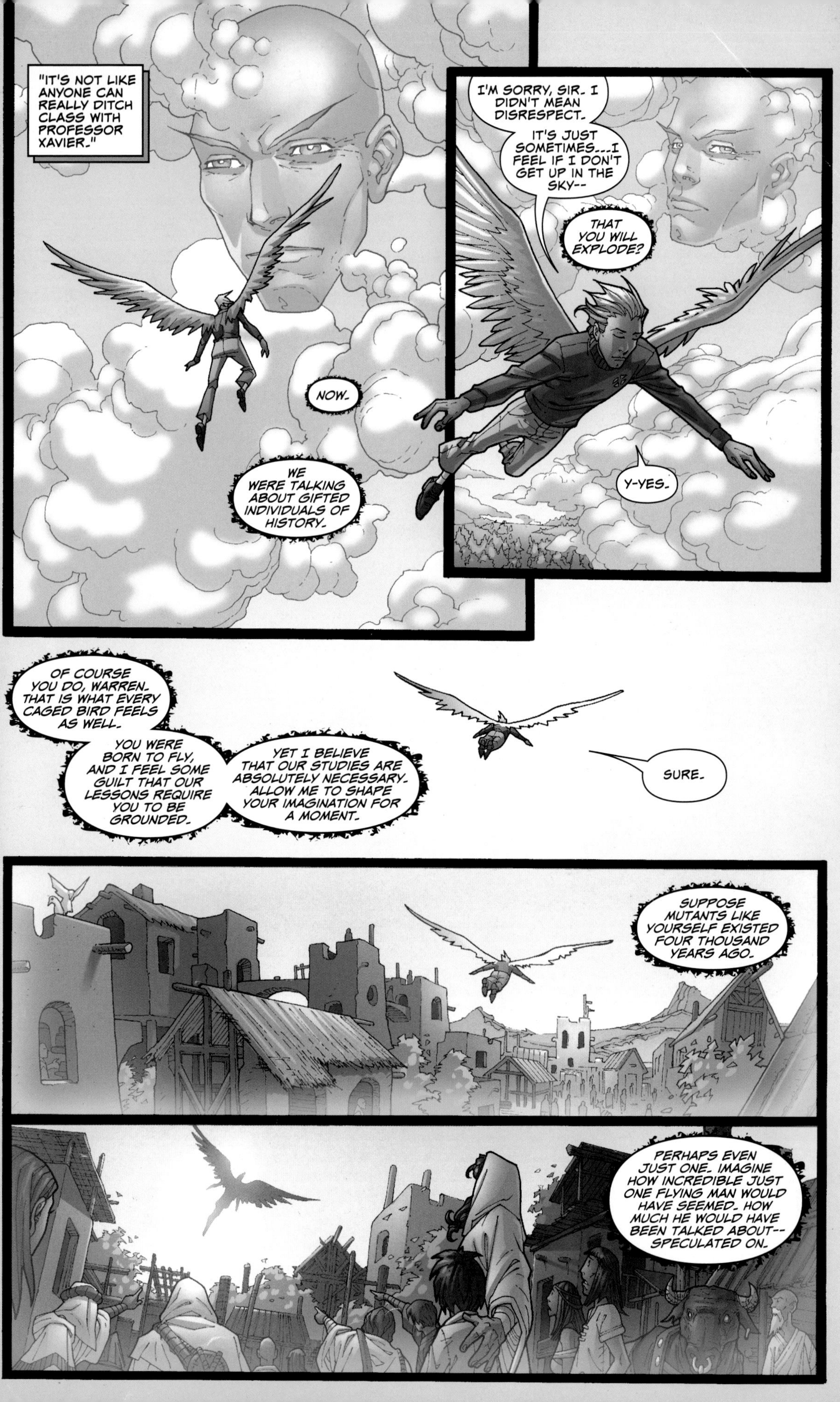
"IT'S NOT LIKE ANYONE CAN REALLY DITCH CLASS WITH PROFESSOR XAVIER."
NOW.
WE WERE TALKING ABOUT GIFTED INDIVIDUALS OF HISTORY.
I'M SORRY, SIR. I DIDN'T MEAN DISRESPECT.
IT'S JUST SOMETIMES... I FEEL IF I DON'T GET UP IN THE SKY--
THAT YOU WILL EXPLODE?
Y-YES.
OF COURSE YOU DO, WARREN. THAT IS WHAT EVERY CAGED BIRD FEELS AS WELL.
YOU WERE BORN TO FLY, AND I FEEL SOME GUILT THAT OUR LESSONS REQUIRE YOU TO BE GROUNDED.
YET I BELIEVE THAT OUR STUDIES ARE ABSOLUTELY NECESSARY. ALLOW ME TO SHAPE YOUR IMAGINATION FOR A MOMENT.
SURE.
SUPPOSE MUTANTS LIKE YOURSELF EXISTED FOUR THOUSAND YEARS AGO.
PERHAPS EVEN JUST ONE. IMAGINE HOW INCREDIBLE JUST ONE FLYING MAN WOULD HAVE SEEMED. HOW MUCH HE WOULD HAVE BEEN TALKED ABOUT--SPECULATED ON.

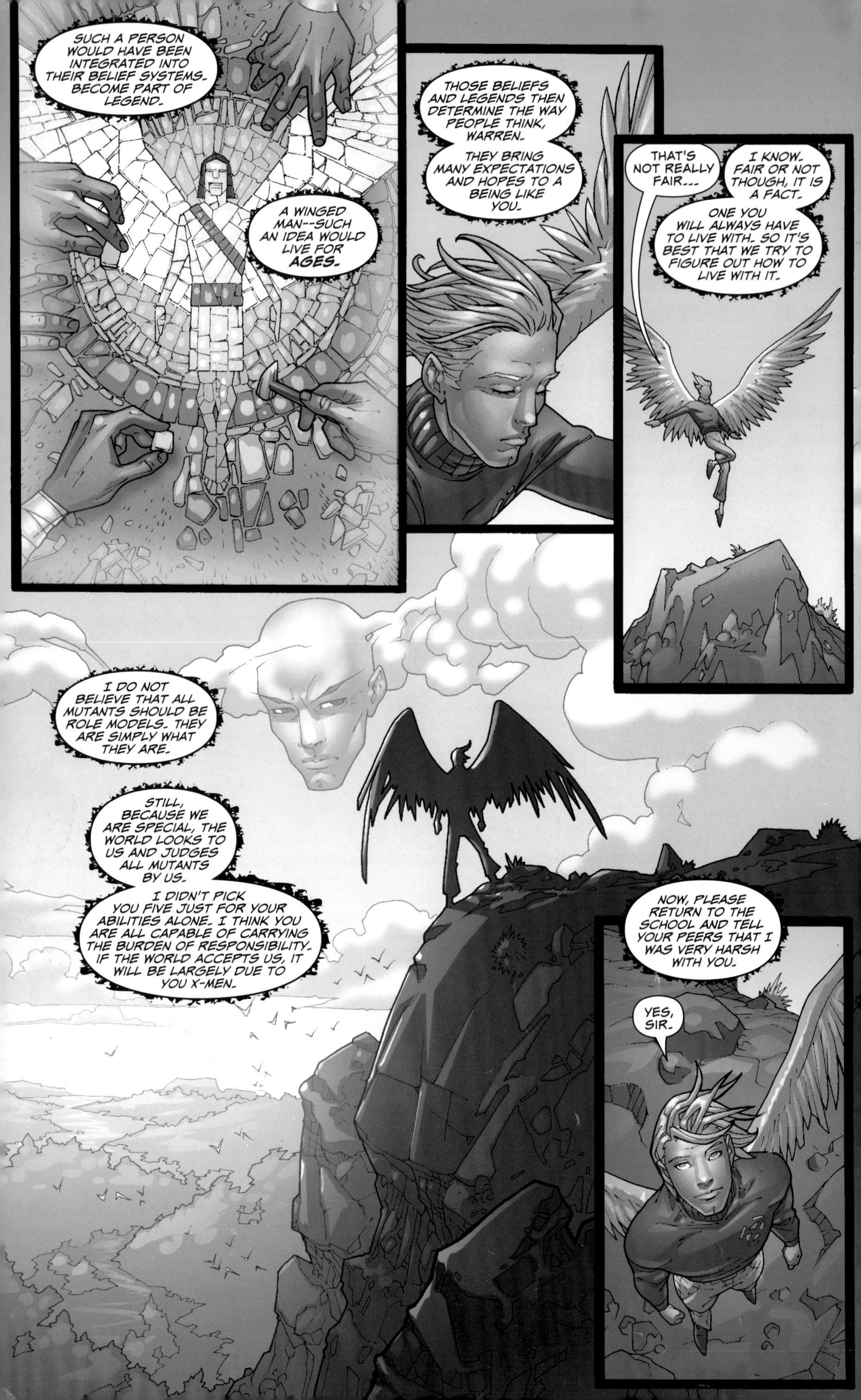
SUCH A PERSON WOULD HAVE BEEN INTEGRATED INTO THEIR BELIEF SYSTEMS. BECOME PART OF LEGEND.
A WINGED MAN--SUCH AN IDEA WOULD LIVE FOR AGES.
THOSE BELIEFS AND LEGENDS THEN DETERMINE THE WAY PEOPLE THINK, WARREN.
THEY BRING MANY EXPECTATIONS AND HOPES TO A BEING LIKE YOU.
THAT'S NOT REALLY FAIR...
I KNOW. FAIR OR NOT THOUGH, IT IS A FACT.
ONE YOU WILL ALWAYS HAVE TO LIVE WITH. SO IT'S BEST THAT WE TRY TO FIGURE OUT HOW TO LIVE WITH IT.
I DO NOT BELIEVE THAT ALL MUTANTS SHOULD BE ROLE MODELS. THEY ARE SIMPLY WHAT THEY ARE.
STILL, BECAUSE WE ARE SPECIAL, THE WORLD LOOKS TO US AND JUDGES ALL MUTANTS BY US.
I DIDN'T PICK YOU FIVE JUST FOR YOUR ABILITIES ALONE. I THINK YOU ARE ALL CAPABLE OF CARRYING THE BURDEN OF RESPONSIBILITY. IF THE WORLD ACCEPTS US, IT WILL BE LARGELY DUE TO YOU X-MEN.
NOW, PLEASE RETURN TO THE SCHOOL AND TELL YOUR PEERS THAT I WAS VERY HARSH WITH YOU.
YES, SIR.

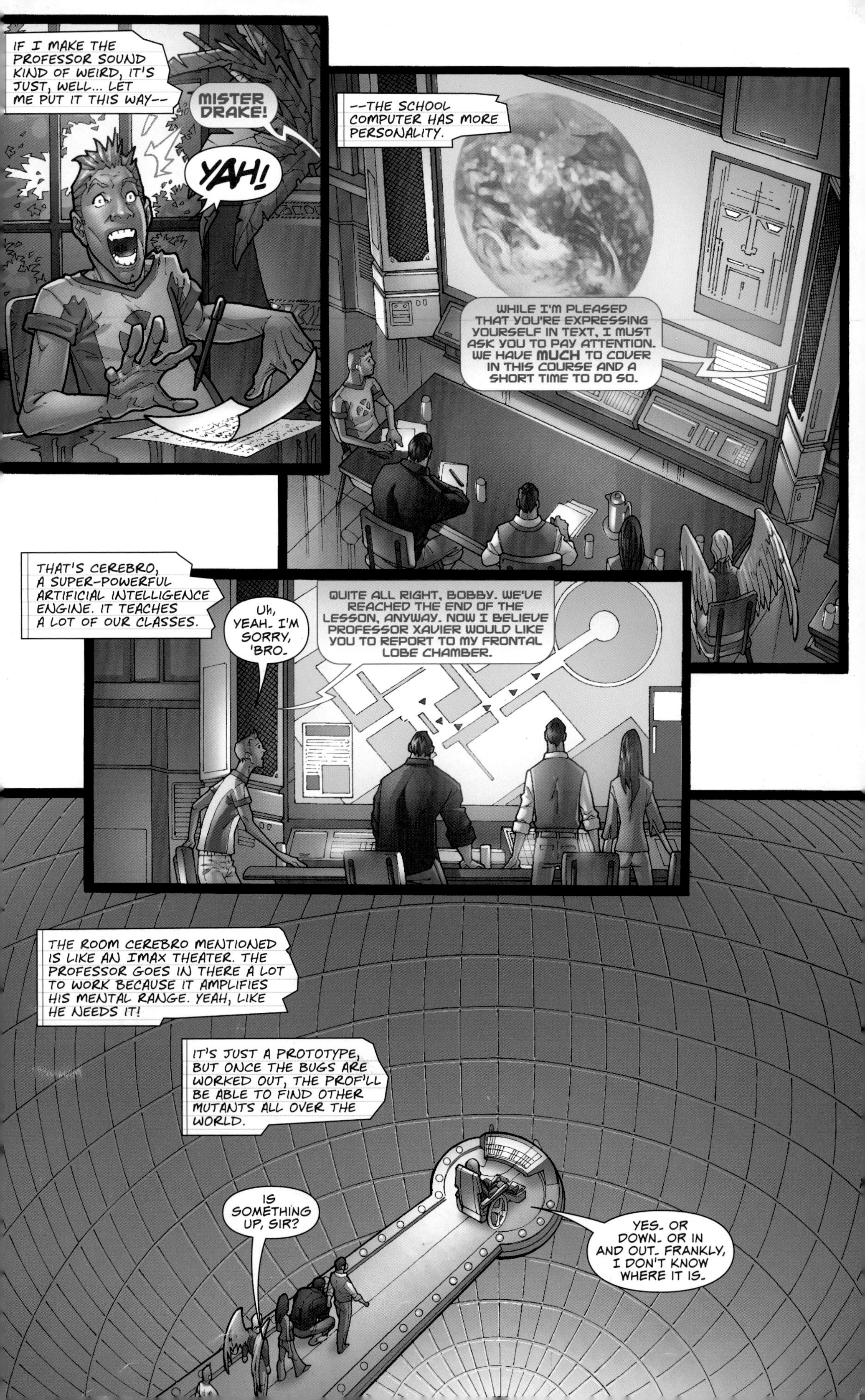
IF I MAKE THE PROFESSOR SOUND KIND OF WEIRD, IT'S JUST, WELL... LET ME PUT IT THIS WAY--
MISTER DRAKE!
YAH!
--THE SCHOOL COMPUTER HAS MORE PERSONALITY.
WHILE I'M PLEASED THAT YOU'RE EXPRESSING YOURSELF IN TEXT, I MUST ASK YOU TO PAY ATTENTION. WE HAVE MUCH TO COVER IN THIS COURSE AND A SHORT TIME TO DO SO.
THAT'S CEREBRO, A SUPER-POWERFUL ARTIFICIAL INTELLIGENCE ENGINE. IT TEACHES A LOT OF OUR CLASSES.
Uh, YEAH. I'M SORRY, 'BRO.
QUITE ALL RIGHT, BOBBY. WE'VE REACHED THE END OF THE LESSON, ANYWAY. NOW I BELIEVE PROFESSOR XAVIER WOULD LIKE YOU TO REPORT TO MY FRONTAL LOBE CHAMBER.
THE ROOM CEREBRO MENTIONED IS LIKE AN IMAX THEATER. THE PROFESSOR GOES IN THERE A LOT TO WORK BECAUSE IT AMPLIFIES HIS MENTAL RANGE. YEAH, LIKE HE NEEDS IT!
IT'S JUST A PROTOTYPE, BUT ONCE THE BUGS ARE WORKED OUT, THE PROF'LL BE ABLE TO FIND OTHER MUTANTS ALL OVER THE WORLD.
IS SOMETHING UP, SIR?
YES. OR DOWN. OR IN AND OUT. FRANKLY, I DON'T KNOW WHERE IT IS.

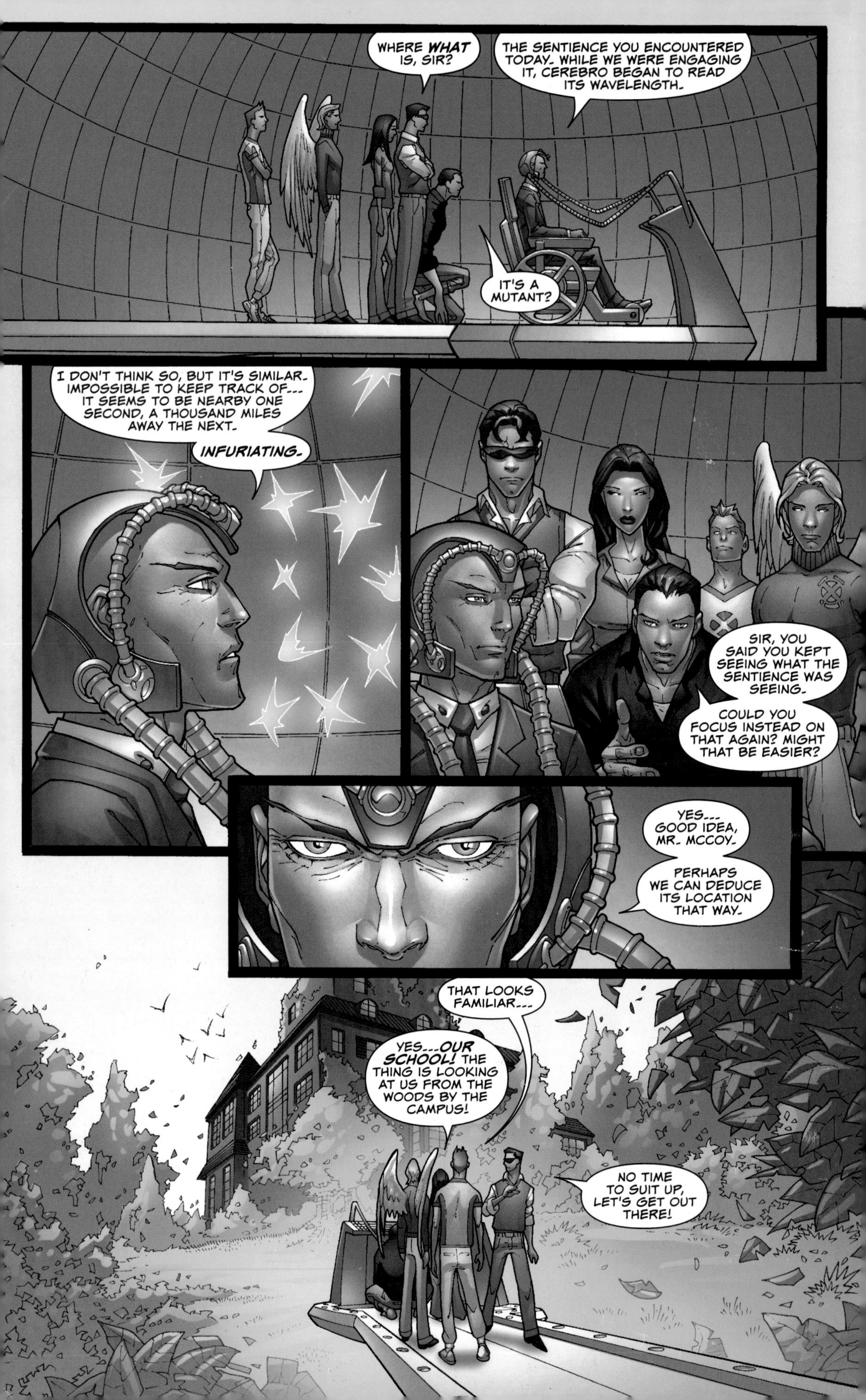
WHERE WHAT IS, SIR?
THE SENTIENCE YOU ENCOUNTERED TODAY. WHILE WE WERE ENGAGING IT, CEREBRO BEGAN TO READ ITS WAVELENGTH.
IT'S A MUTANT?
I DON'T THINK SO, BUT IT'S SIMILAR. IMPOSSIBLE TO KEEP TRACK OF--- IT SEEMS TO BE NEARBY ONE SECOND, A THOUSAND MILES AWAY THE NEXT.
INFURIATING.
SIR, YOU SAID YOU KEPT SEEING WHAT THE SENTIENCE WAS SEEING.
COULD YOU FOCUS INSTEAD ON THAT AGAIN? MIGHT THAT BE EASIER?
YES--- GOOD IDEA, MR. MCCOY.
PERHAPS WE CAN DEDUCE ITS LOCATION THAT WAY.
THAT LOOKS FAMILIAR---
YES---OUR SCHOOL! THE THING IS LOOKING AT US FROM THE WOODS BY THE CAMPUS!
NO TIME TO SUIT UP, LET'S GET OUT THERE!

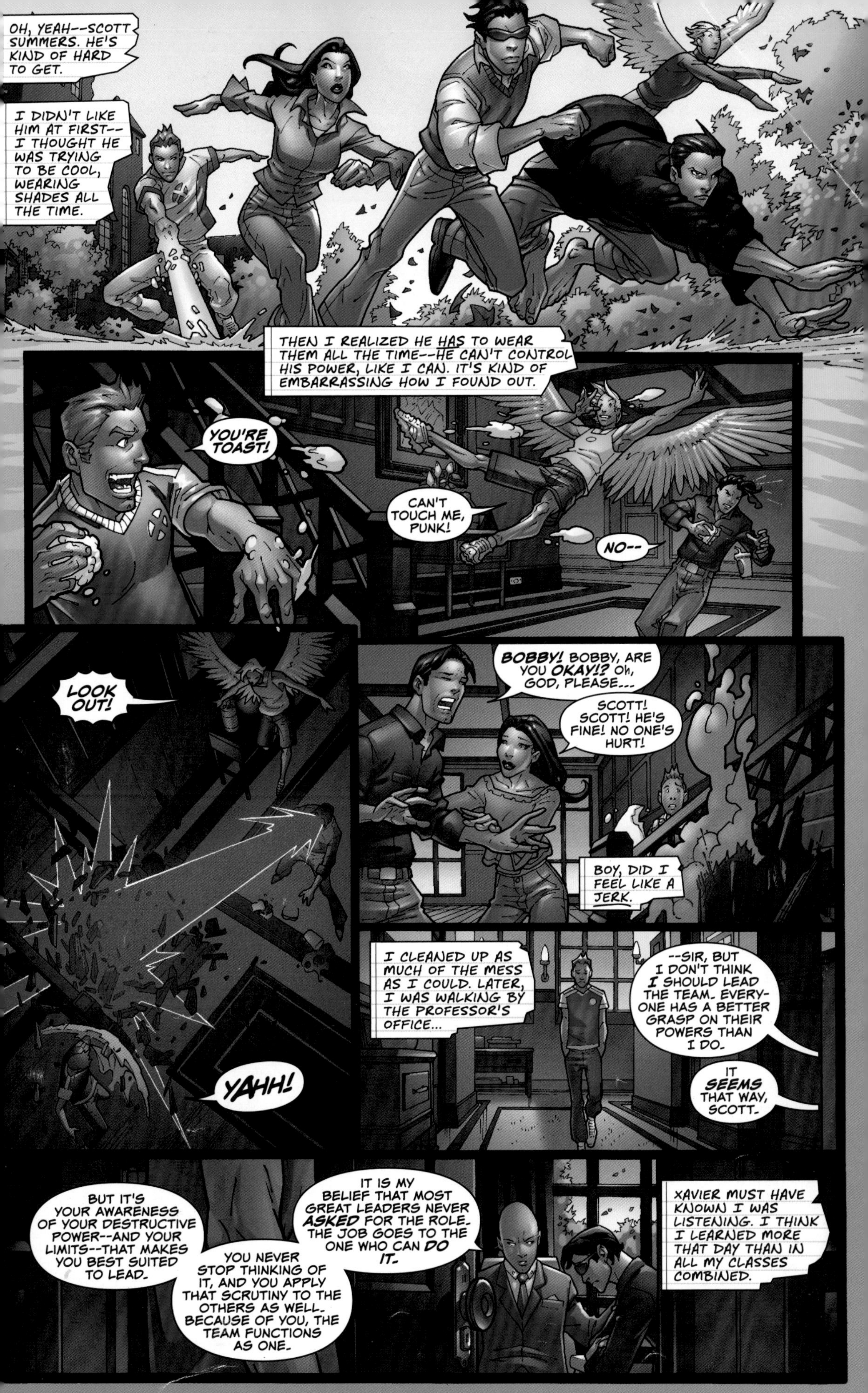

OH, YEAH--SCOTT SUMMERS. HE'S KIND OF HARD TO GET.
I DIDN'T LIKE HIM AT FIRST--I THOUGHT HE WAS TRYING TO BE COOL, WEARING SHADES ALL THE TIME.
THEN I REALIZED HE HAS TO WEAR THEM ALL THE TIME--HE CAN'T CONTROL HIS POWER, LIKE I CAN. IT'S KIND OF EMBARRASSING HOW I FOUND OUT.
YOU'RE TOAST!
CAN'T TOUCH ME, PUNK!
NO--
LOOK OUT!
YAHH!
BOBBY! BOBBY, ARE YOU OKAY!? OH, GOD, PLEASE...
SCOTT! SCOTT! HE'S FINE! NO ONE'S HURT!
BOY, DID I FEEL LIKE A JERK.
I CLEANED UP AS MUCH OF THE MESS AS I COULD. LATER, I WAS WALKING BY THE PROFESSOR'S OFFICE...
--SIR, BUT I DON'T THINK I SHOULD LEAD THE TEAM. EVERYONE HAS A BETTER GRASP ON THEIR POWERS THAN I DO.
IT SEEMS THAT WAY, SCOTT.
BUT IT'S YOUR AWARENESS OF YOUR DESTRUCTIVE POWER--AND YOUR LIMITS--THAT MAKES YOU BEST SUITED TO LEAD.
YOU NEVER STOP THINKING OF IT, AND YOU APPLY THAT SCRUTINY TO THE OTHERS AS WELL. BECAUSE OF YOU, THE TEAM FUNCTIONS AS ONE.
IT IS MY BELIEF THAT MOST GREAT LEADERS NEVER ASKED FOR THE ROLE. THE JOB GOES TO THE ONE WHO CAN DO IT.
XAVIER MUST HAVE KNOWN I WAS LISTENING. I THINK I LEARNED MORE THAT DAY THAN IN ALL MY CLASSES COMBINED.

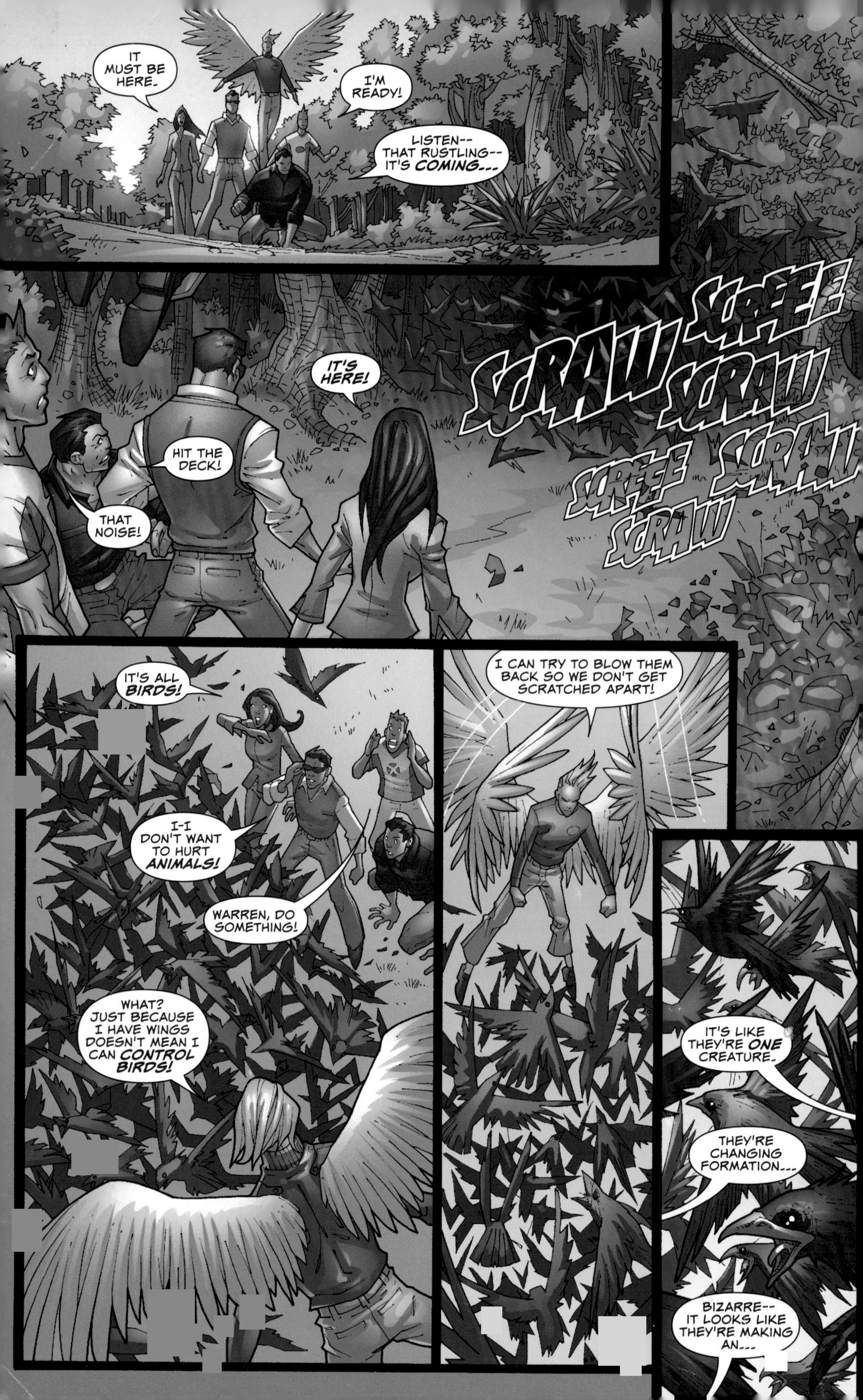
IT MUST BE HERE.
I'M READY!
LISTEN-- THAT RUSTLING-- IT'S COMING...
IT'S HERE!
HIT THE DECK!
THAT NOISE!
SCRAW
SCREEE
SCRAW
SCREEE
SCRAW
SCRAW
IT'S ALL BIRDS!
I-I DON'T WANT TO HURT ANIMALS!
WARREN, DO SOMETHING!
WHAT? JUST BECAUSE I HAVE WINGS DOESN'T MEAN I CAN CONTROL BIRDS!
I CAN TRY TO BLOW THEM BACK SO WE DON'T GET SCRATCHED APART!
IT'S LIKE THEY'RE ONE CREATURE.
THEY'RE CHANGING FORMATION...
BIZARRE-- IT LOOKS LIKE THEY'RE MAKING AN...

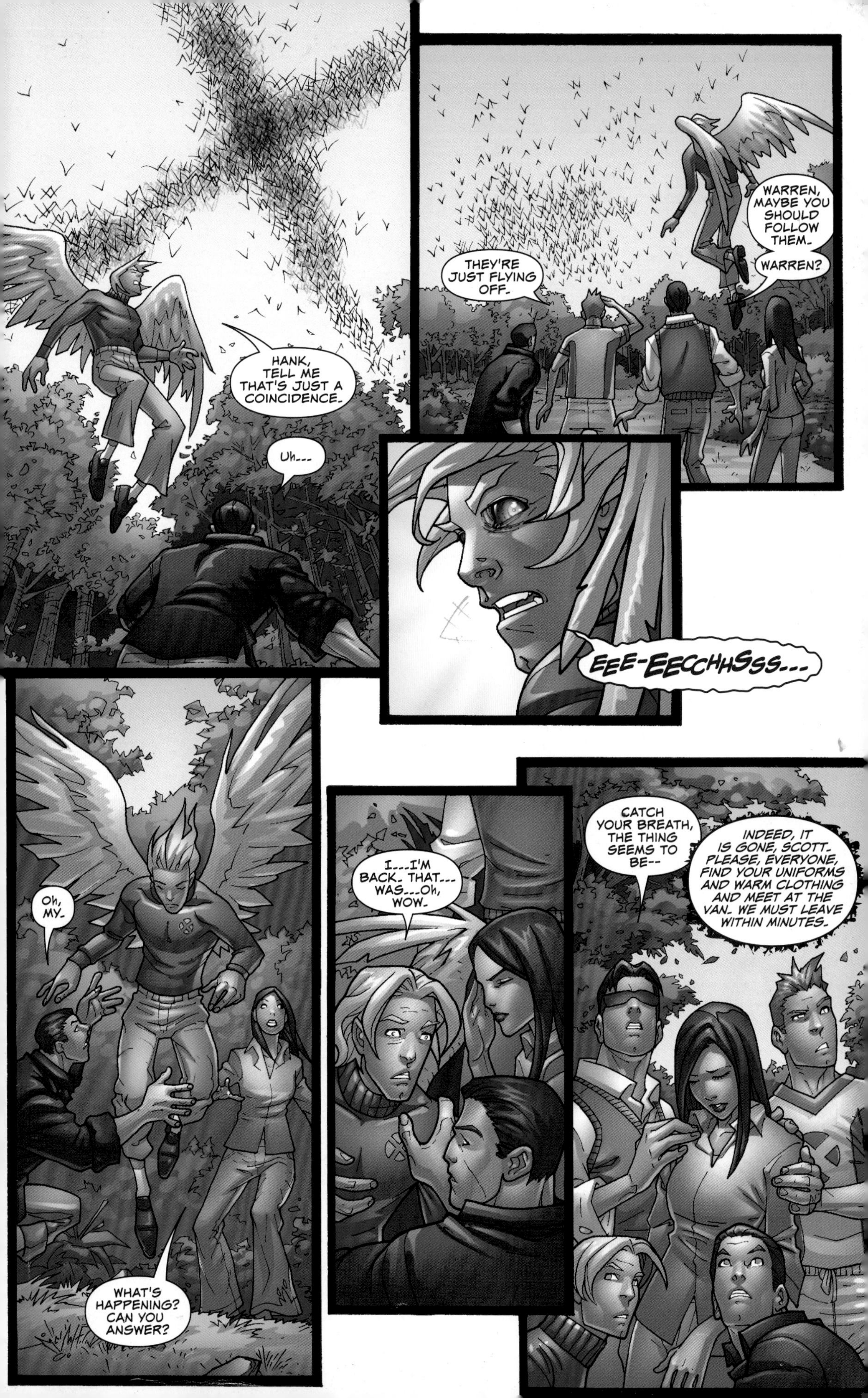
HANK, TELL ME THAT'S JUST A COINCIDENCE.
Uh...
THEY'RE JUST FLYING OFF.
WARREN, MAYBE YOU SHOULD FOLLOW THEM.
WARREN?
EEE-EECCHHSss...
Oh, MY.
WHAT'S HAPPENING? CAN YOU ANSWER?
I...I'M BACK. THAT... WAS...Oh, WOW.
CATCH YOUR BREATH, THE THING SEEMS TO BE--
INDEED, IT IS GONE, SCOTT. PLEASE, EVERYONE, FIND YOUR UNIFORMS AND WARM CLOTHING AND MEET AT THE VAN. WE MUST LEAVE WITHIN MINUTES.

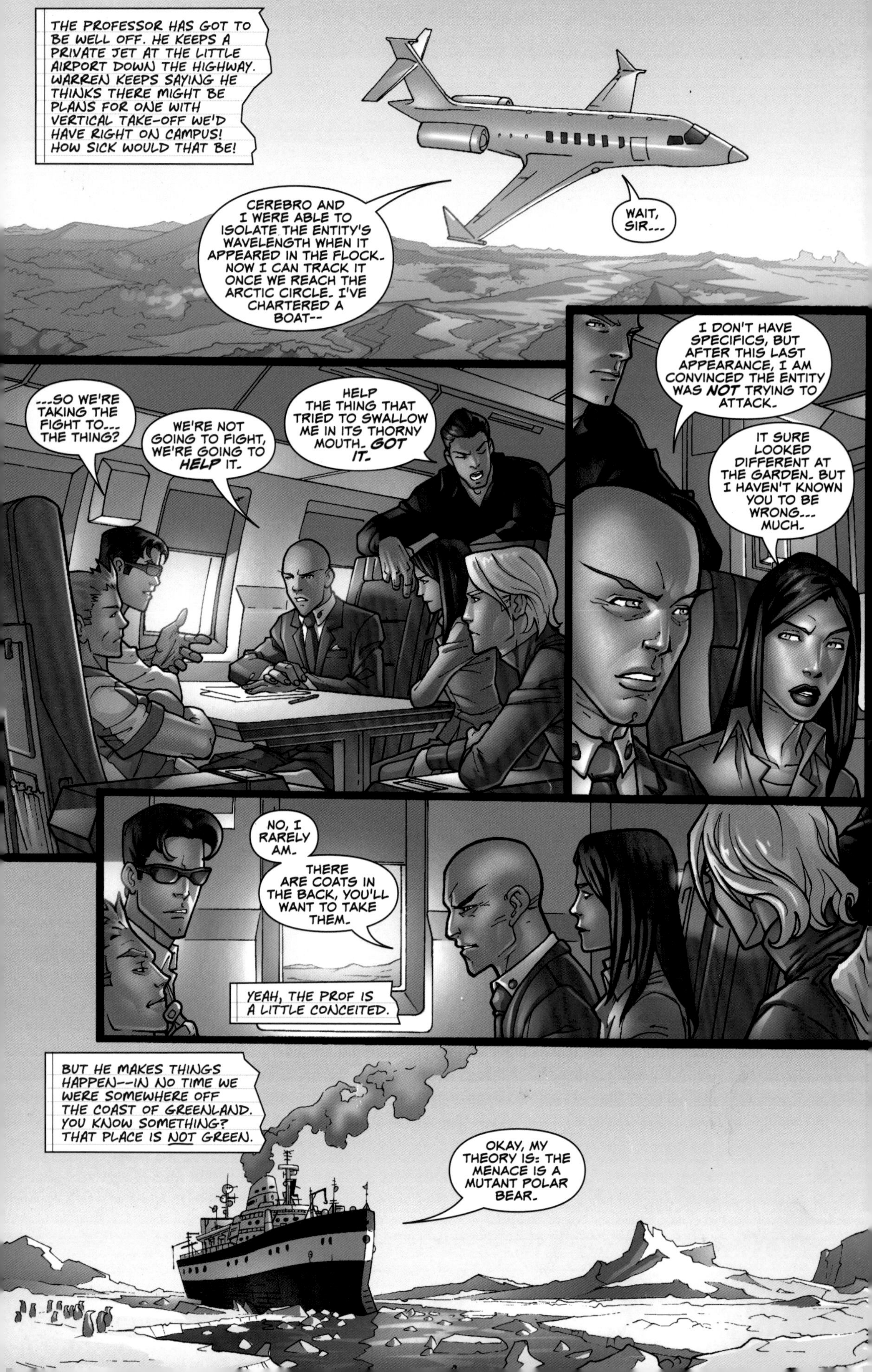
THE PROFESSOR HAS GOT TO BE WELL OFF. HE KEEPS A PRIVATE JET AT THE LITTLE AIRPORT DOWN THE HIGHWAY. WARREN KEEPS SAYING HE THINKS THERE MIGHT BE PLANS FOR ONE WITH VERTICAL TAKE-OFF WE'D HAVE RIGHT ON CAMPUS! HOW SICK WOULD THAT BE!
CEREBRO AND I WERE ABLE TO ISOLATE THE ENTITY'S WAVELENGTH WHEN IT APPEARED IN THE FLOCK. NOW I CAN TRACK IT ONCE WE REACH THE ARCTIC CIRCLE. I'VE CHARTERED A BOAT--
WAIT, SIR...
...SO WE'RE TAKING THE FIGHT TO... THE THING?
WE'RE NOT GOING TO FIGHT, WE'RE GOING TO HELP IT.
HELP THE THING THAT TRIED TO SWALLOW ME IN ITS THORNY MOUTH. GOT IT.
I DON'T HAVE SPECIFICS, BUT AFTER THIS LAST APPEARANCE, I AM CONVINCED THE ENTITY WAS NOT TRYING TO ATTACK.
IT SURE LOOKED DIFFERENT AT THE GARDEN. BUT I HAVEN'T KNOWN YOU TO BE WRONG... MUCH.
NO, I RARELY AM.
THERE ARE COATS IN THE BACK, YOU'LL WANT TO TAKE THEM.
YEAH, THE PROF IS A LITTLE CONCEITED.
BUT HE MAKES THINGS HAPPEN--IN NO TIME WE WERE SOMEWHERE OFF THE COAST OF GREENLAND. YOU KNOW SOMETHING? THAT PLACE IS NOT GREEN.
OKAY, MY THEORY IS: THE MENACE IS A MUTANT POLAR BEAR.

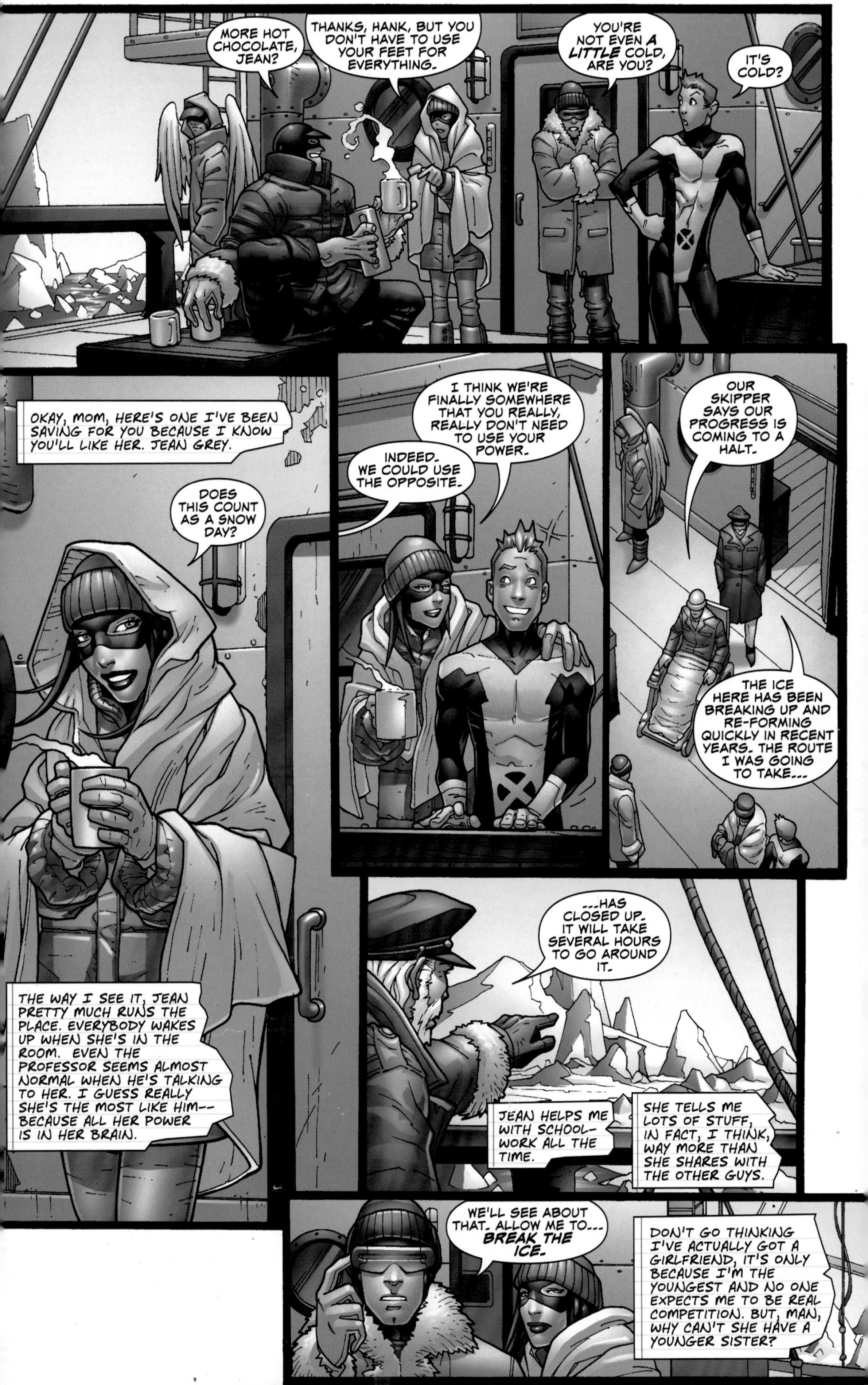
MORE HOT CHOCOLATE, JEAN?
THANKS, HANK, BUT YOU DON'T HAVE TO USE YOUR FEET FOR EVERYTHING.
YOU'RE NOT EVEN A LITTLE COLD, ARE YOU?
IT'S COLD?
OKAY, MOM, HERE'S ONE I'VE BEEN SAVING FOR YOU BECAUSE I KNOW YOU'LL LIKE HER. JEAN GREY.
DOES THIS COUNT AS A SNOW DAY?
I THINK WE'RE FINALLY SOMEWHERE THAT YOU REALLY, REALLY DON'T NEED TO USE YOUR POWER.
INDEED. WE COULD USE THE OPPOSITE.
OUR SKIPPER SAYS OUR PROGRESS IS COMING TO A HALT.
THE ICE HERE HAS BEEN BREAKING UP AND RE-FORMING QUICKLY IN RECENT YEARS. THE ROUTE I WAS GOING TO TAKE...
...HAS CLOSED UP. IT WILL TAKE SEVERAL HOURS TO GO AROUND IT.
THE WAY I SEE IT, JEAN PRETTY MUCH RUNS THE PLACE. EVERYBODY WAKES UP WHEN SHE'S IN THE ROOM. EVEN THE PROFESSOR SEEMS ALMOST NORMAL WHEN HE'S TALKING TO HER. I GUESS REALLY SHE'S THE MOST LIKE HIM--BECAUSE ALL HER POWER IS IN HER BRAIN.
JEAN HELPS ME WITH SCHOOL-WORK ALL THE TIME.
SHE TELLS ME LOTS OF STUFF, IN FACT, I THINK, WAY MORE THAN SHE SHARES WITH THE OTHER GUYS.
WE'LL SEE ABOUT THAT. ALLOW ME TO... BREAK THE ICE.
DON'T GO THINKING I'VE ACTUALLY GOT A GIRLFRIEND, IT'S ONLY BECAUSE I'M THE YOUNGEST AND NO ONE EXPECTS ME TO BE REAL COMPETITION. BUT, MAN, WHY CAN'T SHE HAVE A YOUNGER SISTER?

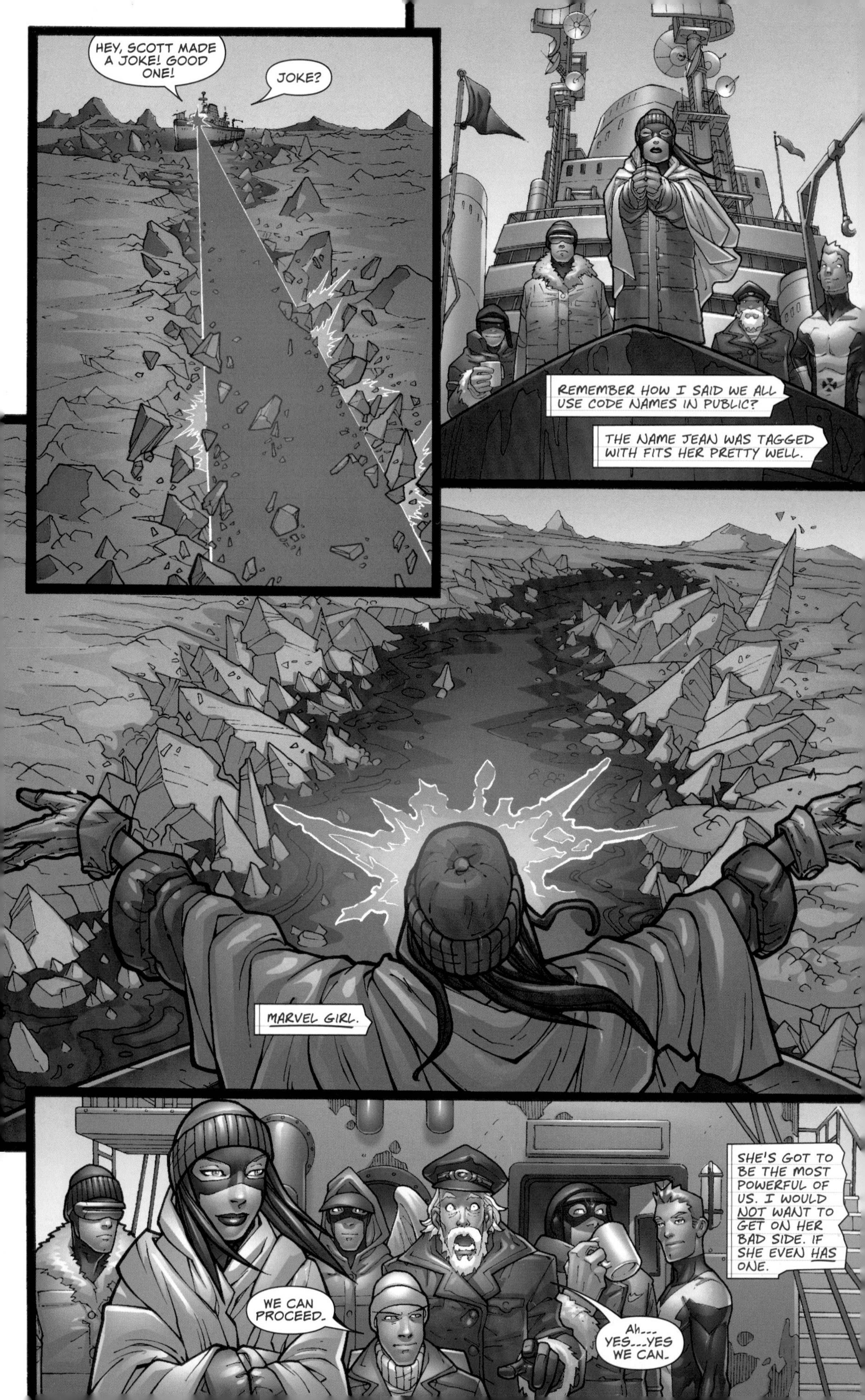
HEY, SCOTT MADE A JOKE! GOOD ONE!
JOKE?
REMEMBER HOW I SAID WE ALL USE CODE NAMES IN PUBLIC?
THE NAME JEAN WAS TAGGED WITH FITS HER PRETTY WELL.
MARVEL GIRL.
SHE'S GOT TO BE THE MOST POWERFUL OF US. I WOULD NOT WANT TO GET ON HER BAD SIDE. IF SHE EVEN HAS ONE.
WE CAN PROCEED.
Ah... YES...YES WE CAN.

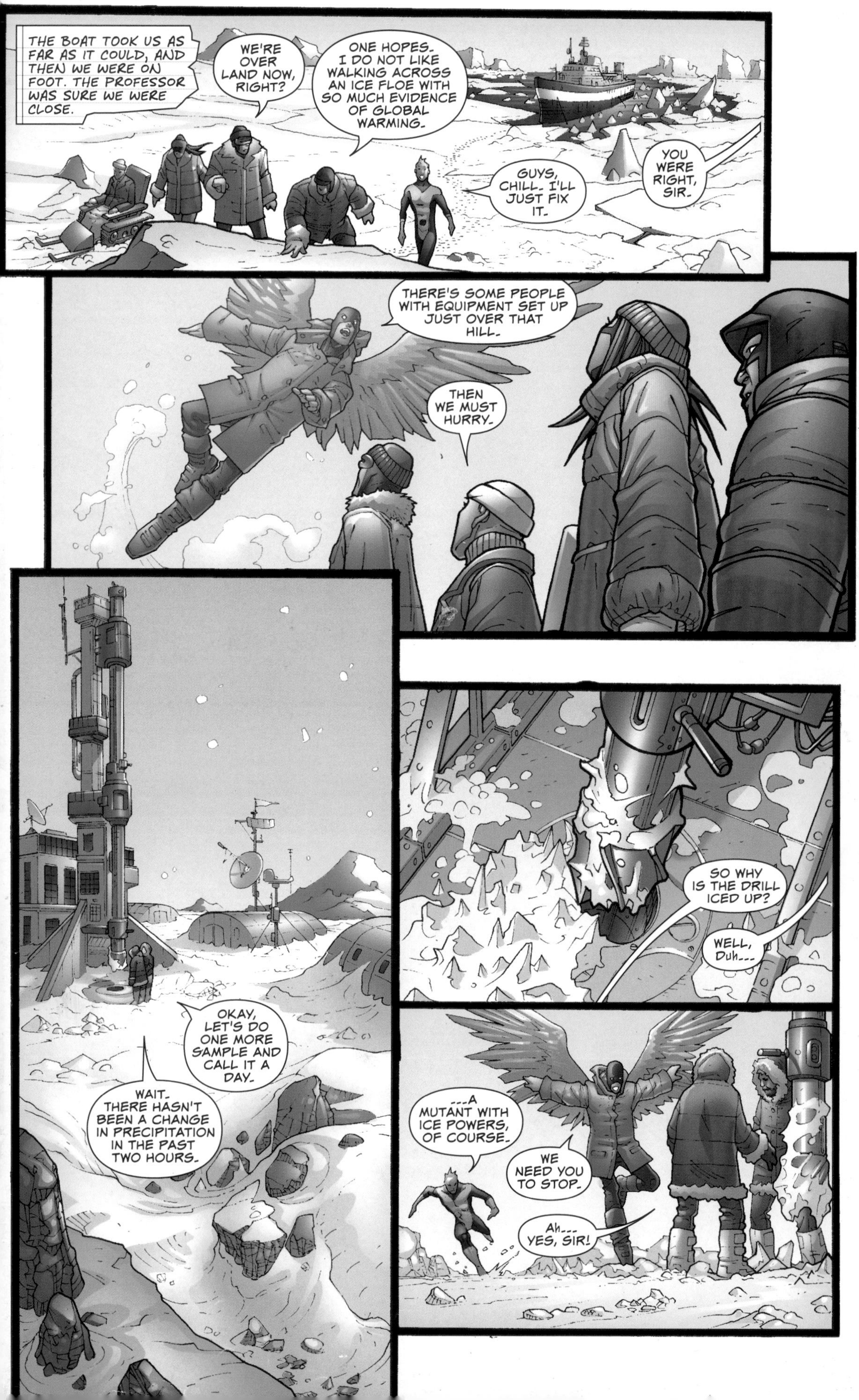
THE BOAT TOOK US AS FAR AS IT COULD, AND THEN WE WERE ON FOOT. THE PROFESSOR WAS SURE WE WERE CLOSE.
WE'RE OVER LAND NOW, RIGHT?
ONE HOPES. I DO NOT LIKE WALKING ACROSS AN ICE FLOE WITH SO MUCH EVIDENCE OF GLOBAL WARMING.
GUYS, CHILL. I'LL JUST FIX IT.
YOU WERE RIGHT, SIR.
THERE'S SOME PEOPLE WITH EQUIPMENT SET UP JUST OVER THAT HILL.
THEN WE MUST HURRY.
OKAY, LET'S DO ONE MORE SAMPLE AND CALL IT A DAY.
WAIT. THERE HASN'T BEEN A CHANGE IN PRECIPITATION IN THE PAST TWO HOURS.
SO WHY IS THE DRILL ICED UP?
WELL, Duh...
...A MUTANT WITH ICE POWERS, OF COURSE.
WE NEED YOU TO STOP.
Ah... YES, SIR!

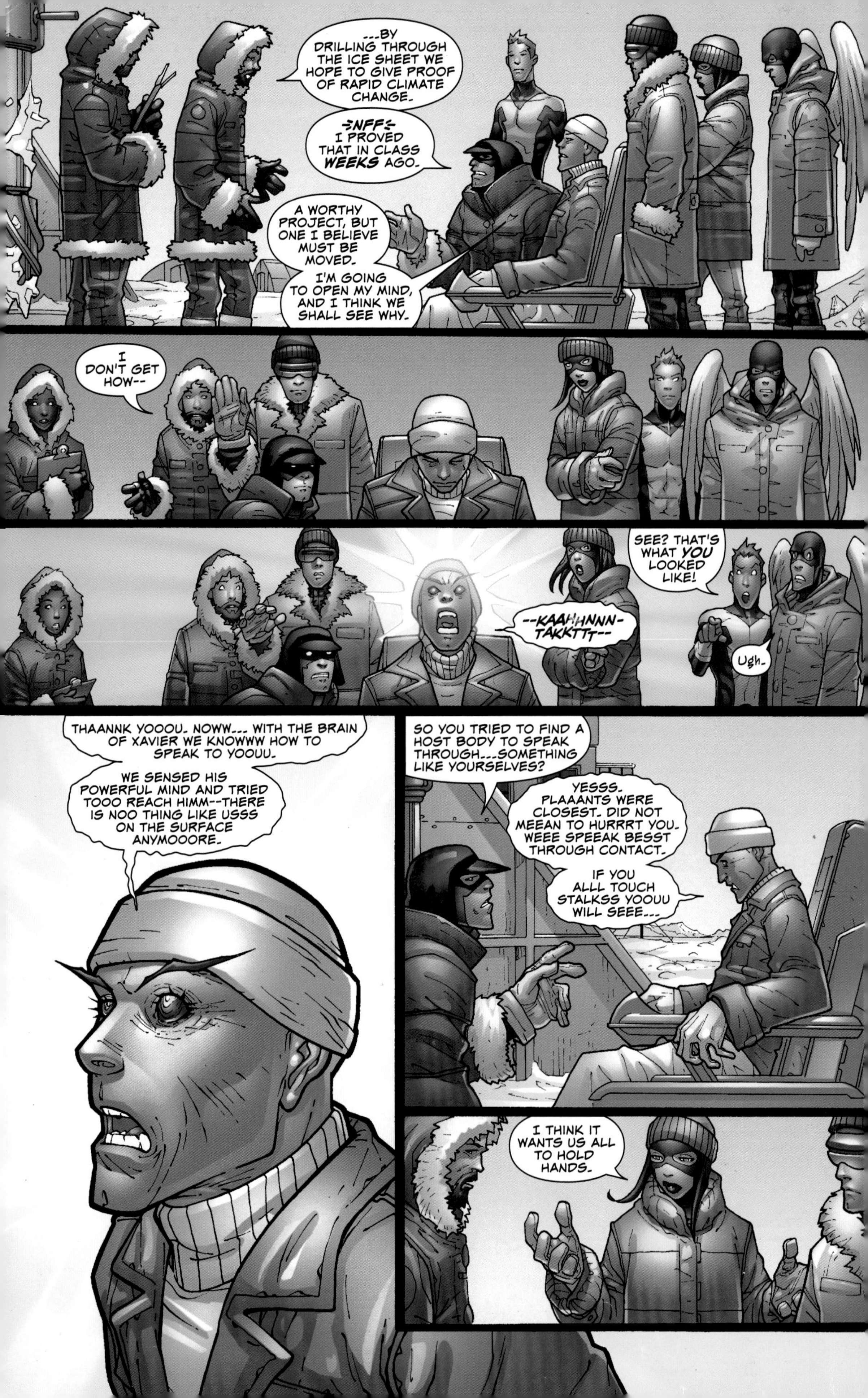
...BY DRILLING THROUGH THE ICE SHEET WE HOPE TO GIVE PROOF OF RAPID CLIMATE CHANGE.
SNFF I PROVED THAT IN CLASS WEEKS AGO.
A WORTHY PROJECT, BUT ONE I BELIEVE MUST BE MOVED.
I'M GOING TO OPEN MY MIND, AND I THINK WE SHALL SEE WHY.
I DON'T GET HOW--
SEE? THAT'S WHAT YOU LOOKED LIKE!
--KAAHHNNN-TAKKTTT--
Ugh.
THAANNK YOOOU. NOWW... WITH THE BRAIN OF XAVIER WE KNOWWW HOW TO SPEAK TO YOOUU.
WE SENSED HIS POWERFUL MIND AND TRIED TOOO REACH HIMM--THERE IS NOO THING LIKE USSS ON THE SURFACE ANYMOOORE.
SO YOU TRIED TO FIND A HOST BODY TO SPEAK THROUGH...SOMETHING LIKE YOURSELVES?
YESSS. PLAAANTS WERE CLOSEST. DID NOT MEEAN TO HURRRT YOU. WEEE SPEEAK BESST THROUGH CONTACT.
IF YOU ALLL TOUCH STALKSS YOOUU WILL SEEE...
I THINK IT WANTS US ALL TO HOLD HANDS.

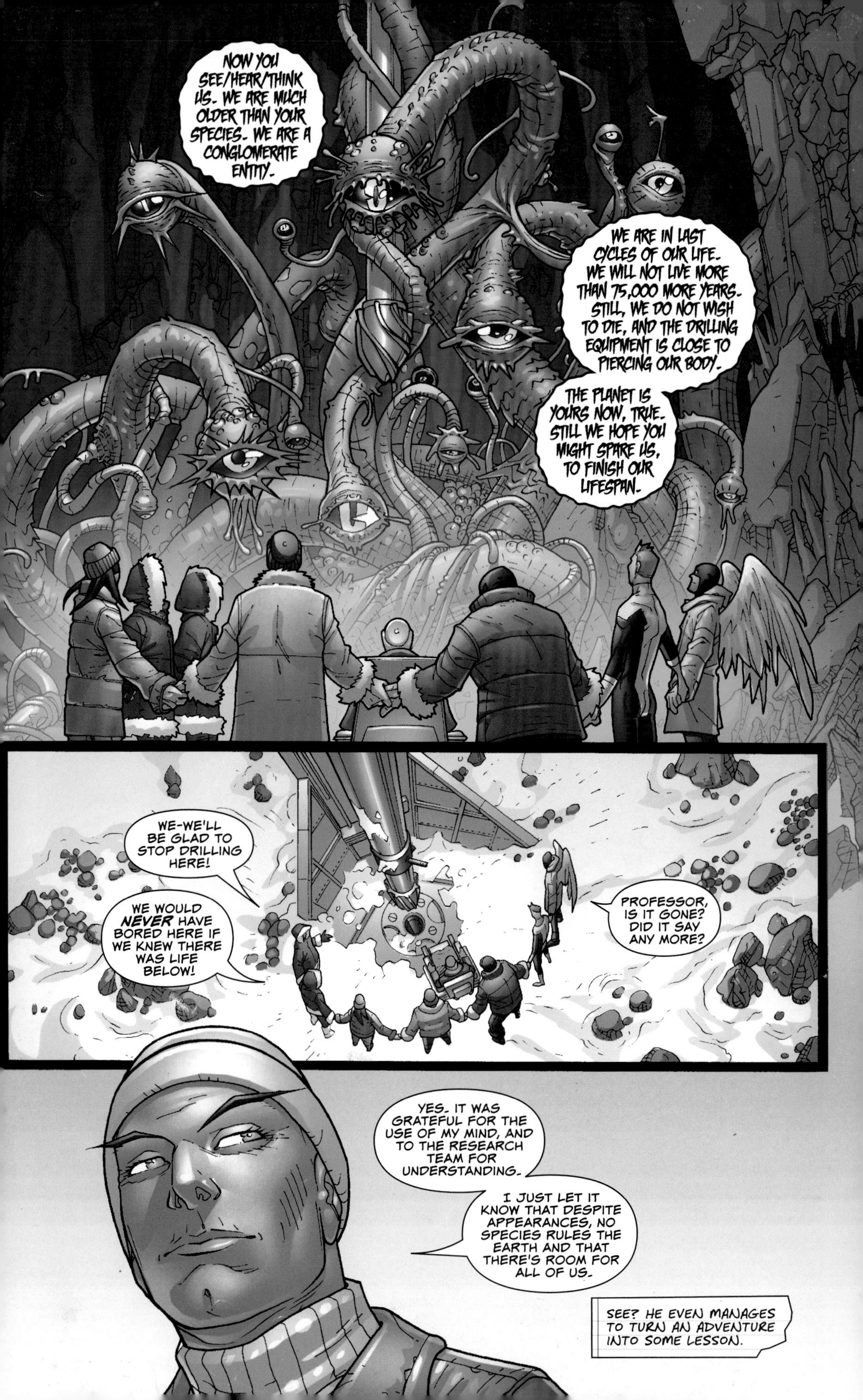
NOW YOU SEE/HEAR/THINK US. WE ARE MUCH OLDER THAN YOUR SPECIES. WE ARE A CONGLOMERATE ENTITY.
WE ARE IN LAST CYCLES OF OUR LIFE. WE WILL NOT LIVE MORE THAN 75,000 MORE YEARS. STILL, WE DO NOT WISH TO DIE, AND THE DRILLING EQUIPMENT IS CLOSE TO PIERCING OUR BODY.
THE PLANET IS YOURS NOW, TRUE. STILL WE HOPE YOU MIGHT SPARE US, TO FINISH OUR LIFESPAN.
WE-WE'LL BE GLAD TO STOP DRILLING HERE!
WE WOULD **NEVER** HAVE BORED HERE IF WE KNEW THERE WAS LIFE BELOW!
PROFESSOR, IS IT GONE? DID IT SAY ANY MORE?
YES. IT WAS GRATEFUL FOR THE USE OF MY MIND, AND TO THE RESEARCH TEAM FOR UNDERSTANDING.
I JUST LET IT KNOW THAT DESPITE APPEARANCES, NO SPECIES RULES THE EARTH AND THAT THERE'S ROOM FOR ALL OF US.
SEE? HE EVEN MANAGES TO TURN AN ADVENTURE INTO SOME LESSON.

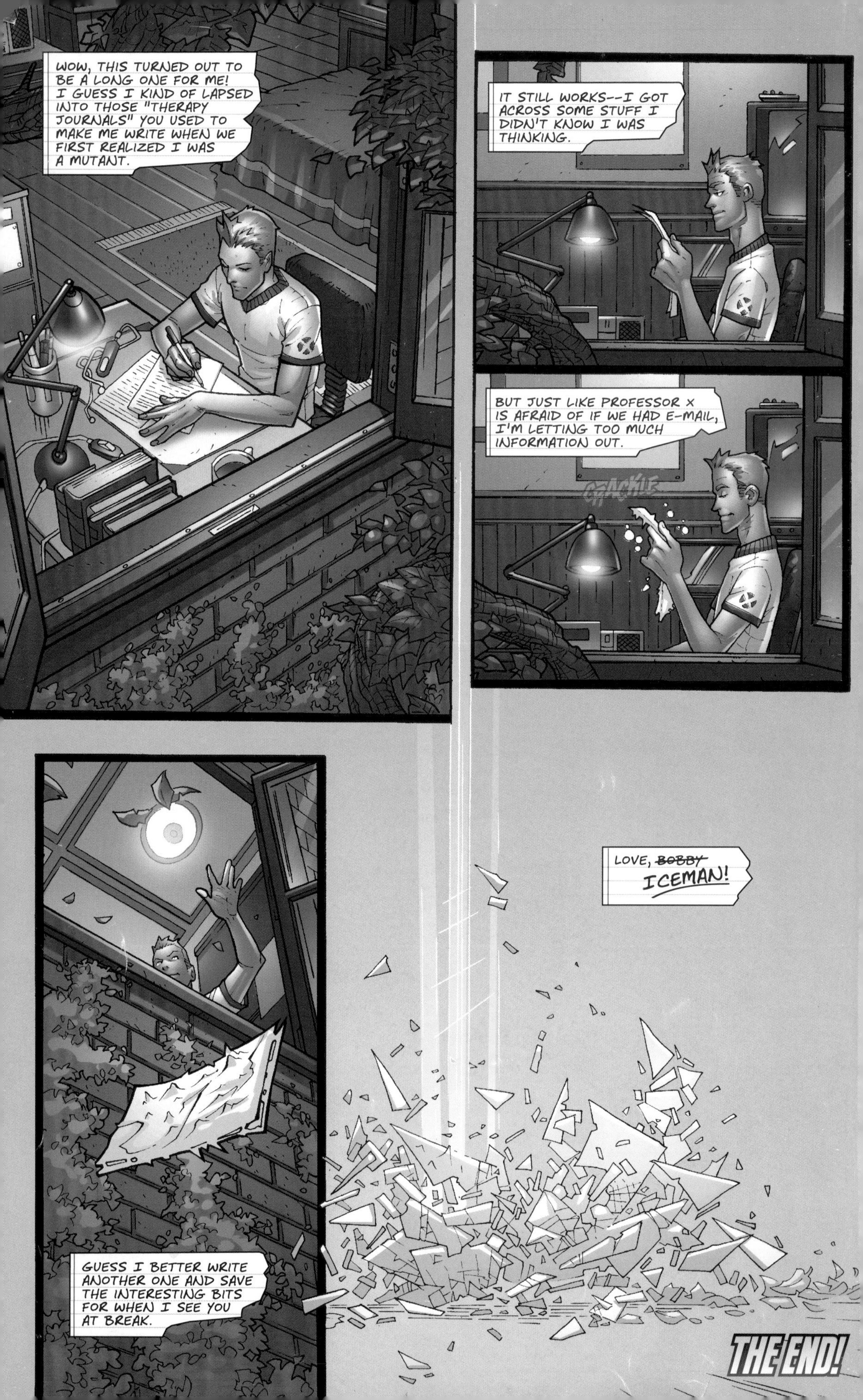
WOW, THIS TURNED OUT TO BE A LONG ONE FOR ME! I GUESS I KIND OF LAPSED INTO THOSE "THERAPY JOURNALS" YOU USED TO MAKE ME WRITE WHEN WE FIRST REALIZED I WAS A MUTANT.
IT STILL WORKS--I GOT ACROSS SOME STUFF I DIDN'T KNOW I WAS THINKING.
BUT JUST LIKE PROFESSOR X IS AFRAID OF IF WE HAD E-MAIL, I'M LETTING TOO MUCH INFORMATION OUT.
CRACKLE
GUESS I BETTER WRITE ANOTHER ONE AND SAVE THE INTERESTING BITS FOR WHEN I SEE YOU AT BREAK.
LOVE, ~~BOBBY~~ ICEMAN!
THE END!